Planting Dreams

A Swedish Immigrant's Journey to America

Planting Dreams

A Swedish Immigrant's Journey to America

Linda K. Hubalek

Butterfield Books, Inc.
Lindsborg, Kansas

Planting Dreams
© 1997 by Linda K. Hubalek

Printed in the United States of America

For details and order blanks for the *Butter in the Well* series, the *Trail of Thread* series, and the *Planting Dreams* series, please see page 105 in the back of this book. If you wish to contact the publisher or author, please address to Book Kansas!/Butterfield Books, Inc., PO Box 407, Lindsborg, KS 67456-0407. Each book is $9.95, plus $3.00 s/h for the first book ordered and $.50 for each additional book.

Consulting Editor: Dianne Russell
Cover Design: Lightbourne Images, copyright 1997
Cover photo courtesy of Don Johnson

Publisher's Cataloging-in-Publication
(Prepared by Quality Books, Inc.)

Hubalek, Linda K.
planting dreams : a Swedish immigrant's journey to America /
Linda K. Hubalek. -- 1st ed.
p. cm. -- (Planting dreams series ; no. one)
Includes bibliographical references.
Preassigned LCCN: 97-92245
ISBN: 1-886652-11-2
1. Immigrants--United States--Fiction 2. Swedes--United States
--Fiction. 3. Frontier and pioneer life--Kansas--Fiction. I. Title.
PS3558.U19P53 1997   813'.54
                                       QB197-40955

To the women who left their homelands
for the betterment of their families

Books by Linda K. Hubalek

Butter in the Well
Prärieblomman
Egg Gravy
Looking Back
Trail of Thread
Thimble of Soil
Stitch of Courage
Planting Dreams
Cultivating Hope (1998)
Harvesting Faith (1999)

Acknowledgments

I would like to express my sincerest thanks to all the family members who helped me trace the journey of our family for *Planting Dreams*. I think we proved that every step our ancestors took toward a new life in America shaped our destiny today.
Tack så mycket.

Linda Katherine Johnson Hubalek

Table of Contents

Foreword

Can you imagine starting a journey to an unknown country without knowing what the country would be like, where you would live, or how you would survive? Was the decision you made to leave the right one?

This first book in the *Planting Dreams* series portrays my great-great grandmother, Charlotta Johnson. The story follows Charlotta and her family as they travel by ship and rail from Sweden in 1868 to their homestead on the opens plains of Kansas a year later.

Only a few pictures and stories of this woman and her family's early years surfaced as I researched this book. Facts and stories have been gleaned from history to give the background of this book, but the bulk is fiction—my version of what it must have been like for Charlotta to leave her home and family in Sweden and face the challenge of starting over in a new land.

And how did this decision affect the rest of Charlotta's life and her children's, and even my life? This three-book series looks at the seasons in Charlotta's life, from her early years to her final days, as I try to answer that question.

I am writing this foreword on May 10, 1997. One hundred and thirty-five years ago today, Samuel Johansson and Charlotta Samuelsdotter were married in Wimmerby, Sweden. Their union, and their decision to immigrate to America, changed the course of their descendant's destiny.

This is how their life, and mine, started on the Kansas prairie.

L. K. H.

The Call West

I woke unusually early this morning but had no desire to burrow deeper under the covers against Samuel's warmth. Last night's discussion after supper haunted my dreams and surfaced the instant sleep cleared from my mind. I needed to get up and away from my husband to think about the questions that keep circling in my head. Even after all these months, I'm still not convinced we have made the right decision.

My warm toes quickly cooled on the plank floor as I hopped to the rug on the hearth. I added wood to the banked coals in the fireplace before dressing in front of it. The nights still cool down the house, even though it is almost April. Wrapping my heavy shawl around my shoulders, I slipped out the door into the ending darkness.

It was too early to start milking, so I walked down the lane and out the farm gate. I wandered through the meadow to where the woods creep to its edges and climbed up the gentle rise. Forests and rocks surround every pocket of farmland that has been cleared in this area. And both are always threatening to reclaim what the farmer has worked so hard to secure.

Without really thinking, I sat down on a large mossy rock where I could view the scenery around me. Although the leaf buds had begun to swell, I could still see through the bare birch trees to the sleeping farm below. The first faint slips of light were filtering into our compound. Gray was giving way to wisps of pink and yellow. Details of the house were becoming clearer as I sat in the silence.

Tufts of fresh grass rim the meadow, but there isn't an overall hint of green as there should be this time of year. The lack of fall rain and winter snow has depleted the soil's moisture and it doesn't have the strength to give its spring burst of color. Will nature change its course and provide abundant moisture for a good crop this season, or will it continue as last year? Samuel has decided we must not wait for nature to decide our fate.

There are eight buildings on the farm built around a square, and all face into the middle. There is a place for everything we need to sustain life. The buildings were constructed in this cluster to protect against the elements. Built of local timbered wood, most of the buildings look weather-beaten. Some shelters have a sod roof, others are thatched. The newer ones are covered with wooden shingles.

The hayloft sits on the northeast corner between the threshing barn on the north and the house on the east. The storage cellar is just south out the door from the house, with the privy to the left of it. On the west side of the farmyard is the cowshed, forage barn, and the woodshed. Narrow roads between the main buildings go out in all four directions from the middle. Outside the square is the summer cowshed on the edge of the meadow, a forage barn, smithy, and the well.

The original farm was called Kulla, but by now it has been divided into four sections. It is located in the Pelarne parish in Kalmar *Län*. The farm was split to support the first son's family, and then again in each succeeding generation.

We are living on the part of Kulla that was owned by my husband's parents. Originally painted a dark red, the house is a *parstuga*, having two large rooms with a small hall and chamber rooms between the two.

Samuel's father, Johannes Samuelsson, came from Lönneberga in 1812 to work for Petter Jonsson, then he married one of Petter's daughters, Anna Greta Pettersdotter, in 1817. They received a quarter acreage from a half of the original farm,—in other words, an eighth of the original Kulla. They built this farm compound over time. On this place they had ten children, five of whom reached maturity.

Now their children have grown and gone their separate ways.

According to custom, the oldest son, Carl Peter, should have inherited the farm from his father, and the other children were to leave home as soon as they were old enough to find employment. But Carl Peter gave up his rights and now owns and operates an ironworks shop instead. Bror August was not interested either, and Johan Anders never married. The youngest, Maria Christina, works as a maid nearby.

That left to Samuel, the fourth son, the chance to farm this land. We were married six years ago and moved in with his parents.

Undantag Johannes has reserved rights, meaning that even though he is a retired farmer who has given up his land, he and his second wife may live in a spare room in the house and receives a share of the farm produce to live on. Johannes is also a churchwarden for our parish, so he is a prominent person in the community.

It is cold among the trees. Little patches of snow still skirt the north side of a few tree trunks. I pull my shawl over my head to cut the chill that penetrates my ears. Spring is around the corner, but it needs the morning sunshine to chase away the chill.

It was partly out of habit that I headed outside early this morning and partly out of need to put everything in perspective.

No matter where we lived that particular year, my sisters and I would head out to the woods very early spring and sit quietly to listen for our destiny. First it was just Carolina and me, giggling nervously at dawn. Then Hedda joined us three years later as soon as she was old enough to catch up with us. Later came Mathilda, whom we took with us as a toddler because we thought she should be in on the tradition. The last siblings joined in as soon as they were old enough.

It is an old Swedish custom to listen for the first call of the *gök* in the spring. Its call tells you what will happen to you in the next year. The cuckoo bird only calls from the first sign of spring until the first cut of the hay, and then it doesn't speak again until the next spring.

You must sit quietly to discern the direction of his call in order to find your answer. A call coming from the west brings the best tidings; a call from the east means comfort and consolation. A call from the north or south means that sorrow and death lie in wait for the listener. After we heard the call, we would conjure up all sorts of guesses as to what the new year would bring. Of course half the time we couldn't agree on what direction the call came from, so that made for interesting conversation. We thought good tidings always meant a boy being interested in one of us. Marriage proposals loomed in our minds as we grew older. We tried not to hear a call from the north or south because we didn't want to face the possibility of a death in our family.

When we lost baby sister, Helena, I thought back to our first spring day that year before she was born and wondered which direction the *gök* call come from. It is just a superstitious thing, but it made me wonder back to that year's outing. It was six years ago, and the last time we would all make this outing together. Carolina and I were both getting married and moving to our husbands' homes. Hedda was soon moving out of the house to work as a maid. Moder was about to deliver her seventh child.

We all heard the call from the north but made excuses. We didn't want to believe the call would mean that death would follow us soon.

Carolina and I both married on the same day, June 10. I married Samuel Fredrik Johansson and transferred my belongings to Kulla.

Carolina moved in with her husband, Gustaf Otto Jonsson, to Gebo, where he inherited his father's farm. Two years later he died, leaving Carolina with a one-year-old girl. But she has since remarried to Johan Erik Jonsson, who moved onto the Gebo farm, and they have had a daughter.

Moder delivered Helena Maria on June 20, but the little girl lived just beyond a year.

We know the deaths had nothing to do with the bird's prediction, but it has always been a sign to consider, no matter our age or where we heard it.

Until I married at eighteen, I was the daughter of *arrendator* Samuel Amundsson, a tenant farmer who had never owned his own land. He and my *moder*, Anna Lena Nilsdotter, have spent their entire lives tending other people's land. The little tenant houses we lived in were crowded with all of us, and we always wished for better, but we knew life would never change. We would always be poor farmers working for others.

We lived in several places as I grew up. Fader was first a servant at Grönshult, where he and Moder were married. My oldest sister, Carolina, was born at Södra Wi, Hedda and I at Rumskulla. The next four, Mathilda, Carl Johan, Sofia, and Helena, were born at Wimmerby, although on two different farms. Sometimes they were better land and houses, sometimes worse. We children didn't know why we moved so often. It was the only way of life we knew. We didn't understand the reasons behinds good years and bad, crop failures and taxes due.

Fader paid his rent with cash. So in years where we had a drought, like last year, he didn't have enough crops to sell to pay the landowner—or the tax man. Moder had to watch her favorite milk cow being taken away this winter because there was no money to pay the taxes.

Carolina was Moder's helper, but I was Fader's, because there were no sons among the oldest children. I tagged along while we tended the animals, worked in the fields, and gathered the harvest. I carried out enough rocks from all those farm fields each spring to build my own castle.

I thought life would be better as a farm owner's wife instead of a tenant farmer's daughter, but we still have debts to worry about and mouths to feed. The fields will never be clear of stones, nor will my castle be built. My lot in life will be the same as my parents. Except that we have decided to leave our homeland and venture to another. Next month we are sailing to America and leaving this rocky land forever.

We talked late last night with Johannes and Stina Kajsa. They know our reasons for wanting to leave, but they have been trying to persuade us to change our minds. We are leaving behind the old generation to help the new one. We all know the reasons why, but it does not ease the pain of the permanent separation coming soon. "This place was good enough for us and you children. Why isn't it good enough for you? The weather changes every year and you know there will always be good years mixed in with the bad. You are the only son that wanted this farm. Now you want to give that up?"

When Samuel and Johannes argue back and forth, Stina and I sit and listen. Johannes is arguing because he knows he will lose his son and grandchildren forever, but he doesn't want to beg Samuel to stay. It looks bad that the churchwarden's son is leaving the parish. Samuel argues because he wants to be a free man— free from his father, his debts, and this land.

Many people from the area are moving to America this spring. Why shouldn't we be among them? There are vast amounts of free land overseas. Why should we stay here and keep pushing these rocks around? What happens when we run out of food for us and the livestock? How are we going to survive?

Questions on the subject of emigration have circulated through the parish all winter as people try to find answers to this dire situation. *Amerikafeber* is catching on with the young people in our parish. There are six families and a dozen single servants already preparing to leave our parish next week. The pull of hope for something better is always catching. You can be rich in America! Why not leave everything behind for a better life in the land of opportunity?

We have listened to the emigrant agents that are always trying to sell tickets for the ship liners heading for America. Ever since the steamships replaced the sailing ships of the old days, ships have left the major ports of Sweden three times a week for America. The agent's job is to fill each ship to capacity. They come to our area regularly, holding meetings wherever they can assemble a crowd. Samuel picks up written information at every meeting and pores over it in the light of the evening fire.

American railroads have also campaigned actively to attract settlers to their land. They hire Swedes who have moved to America to come back to the Old Country to recruit people and escort them overseas.

America's Civil War has ended, and stories of the vast lands available in the newly opened western territories have spread across the sea to us. The Homestead Act gives people land free for the asking. All we would have to do is build a house, clear five acres, and live in it for five years. The way people talk, plowing American soil would be like cutting warm butter with a dull knife compared to our stony earth. As for the five-year stipulation, after we leave this country and obtain land, why would we want to move again?

"Cheap fare to the land of plenty. You can get a job by just standing on a street corner in New York. Food is abundant and cheap. You'll never go hungry again!" claims the agent. But we know he is trying to make a living himself, and many of these agents have never set foot on the faraway soil they are trying to sell. Can we believe their tales of happy endings?

Old newspapers from the big towns circulate around the community. When Samuel obtains one he reads out loud its reprinted letters sent from people who had moved to America. They describe their adventures with sumptuous word pictures, anxious to justify their journey and to rest their worried parents' minds. "The trip only took three weeks and I found work as soon as I was on land. I make four dollars a day, get free room and board at my job, and am free to do as I please on Sunday."

Are they telling the truth, or are they trying to make mask their homesickness by exaggerating their accomplishments? Most people think the writers were bragging, not admitting the real hardships they are encountering. Even though people are skeptical, they read and reread the letters describing America. Everyone is envious of the writers' daring escapes from our country's poverty.

The person who convinced me there might be a better life in America was a son of a poor neighbor who came home after being gone for six years. To escape a bad master, he had fled to the port of Göteborg and signed up as a sailor on a boat heading for America. Upon arriving in America he worked for the Union government during the Civil War, then homesteaded land on the western prairie. He came back to visit his parents and to convince his sweetheart to return to America as his bride.

None of us recognized him at first. In Sweden a person's station in life is identified by his occupation, manner of speech, and form of dress. He had left our district in homespun rags, woolen cap, and wooden shoes. This young man returned in a store-bought suit, a handsome hat, and boots of fine leather. He left with no money in his pocket but returned as the owner of 160 American acres, which he said was larger than most of the estates in our parish. What made me a believer in his story was that he did not bow or back away when he met a member of the gentry on the way to church one Sunday. Instead, he held out his hand to shake the other man's hand because he considered himself an equal, not a servant of the past.

He said there are no class divisions in America. The large-farm holder, sheriff, or pastor is no different from anyone else. Your lowly occupation does not limit you. One person is just as good as another. If you work hard at any honest occupation you are respected. Anyone can save money and own their own farm or store in due time. The fact that women are called either Miss or Mrs. in America sounds good to me. Here there are four different ways to address a married woman, according to her social rank, and the same applies to an unmarried woman. Before I married, *piga*, meaning maidservant, always preceded my name. My station in Sweden may never be higher than it is now.

I sit in the numbing cold, thinking of last year's heat and drought. Trying to survive last year was difficult. Last spring started with optimism as we worked and planted the fields. The thin topsoil was turned along with the little rocks that continue to work their way to the surface. Samuel tried to ignore the telltale signs warning of no moisture in the soil, and he planted the precious seeds that were supposed to turn our lives around. Our emotions changed later to concern and despair over the shriveling crop and dwindling grain storage. Our fields depended on moisture from the sky, but it only produced hot winds. Every night I prayed it would rain, but I never got the answer I needed. The rocky soil absorbed the unusually high temperatures and the intense sun baked the crust so hard that a spade couldn't chip it, let alone a tender seedling penetrate it. We couldn't deny the damage that was progressing daily.

I struggled to keep the garden alive. Seeds we had saved and planted had to grow into food for the family. What were we going to eat during the snowy winter months if these plants didn't mature? I hauled and poured buckets of water on the garden, hoping that the remaining plants had enough energy to produce tubers below the ground or fruit above. My hunger for something ripe and juicy to eat was put down each morning as I viewed the damage done by the hordes of insects intent on eating anything green. I took my frustration out by smashing potato bugs, but it didn't cure my bitterness or their enormous population.

As the summer went on, bewilderment turned into disappointment. Then I was disgusted that neither Samuel nor I could prevent or change our situation, and I was angry that life was so hard for us. We were two young people starting a new life together. I wanted this farm to prosper, to yield abundance for our future.

We needed a crop desperately, but the weather did not moderate. There is no extra grain or money in reserve to fall back on if we stay and have another failure. And with no crops, we won't have money for taxes or food. We finally had to face the fact that we can't change what is happening on our farm and in our country. And if we lose this farm, our four-year-old son, Oscar, will never be more than a servant—as would be the lot for our two-year-old Emilia. And how many more mouths must we be able to feed in the future?

We exhausted ourselves trying to find a solution. We couldn't lose hope because we had two small children depending on us. Finally we have hope for another chance—we can start over in America and it will provide us will everything we ever dreamed of.

Discussions have led to arguments, then back to discussions. Sometimes one of us is for the idea and the other against, then we switch sides. Whether we want them or not, we hear the opinions of other people. Whether it's right or wrong, we don't want it to cloud our judgment. Yes, we are young, but this must to be our decision. We have to live with it for the rest of our lives. Should we wait another year and hope for better weather, or leave now before we get more in debt? It would take a very good crop to pay off our bills and give us food and money to last for the rest of this year.

If we decide to wait a few more years, will there still be land in America, or will it all be given away before we get there? What happens to us if we get there and can't find land, or they stop giving it away? How do we make a living? How will we finance the trip and have money to start over? We don't own much, so we don't have much to sell.

What is the current cost for the ship passage? Will we survive the trip? What about sickness on board and sea storms? How long does it take to get to America?

How much extra money do we need for train or wagon transportation, for food and board along the way? Where are we going to settle once we get to America? Can we get land near the boat dock, or do we have to go west? How far west? What kind of grains can we grow there? Is it different from here, and will we know how to plant and harvest it?

We can't speak English. The questions and obstacles grow every day. Questions have been flooding our house, spoken and unspoken, for months.

Every December 12 we pour new-brewed ale on the roots of the *vårdträd* in memory of our ancestors who lived and died on this farm. This ancestral tree in front of the house has become Samuel's solitary thinking post. He stands out there many nights asking his mother what to do, arguing with a ghost as he tries to find the answer.

My searching thoughts have been part of my everyday tasks as I take care of the children, the cooking and cleaning. Rarely have I had a moment like this to concentrate on the decision that faces us.

My concerns have been different from Samuel's. I am confident he can provide for us with some form of employment, at least temporarily, until we find a farm. But I can't decide if I am strong enough to leave our parents and sisters and brothers behind. We may never venture back to Sweden again. My head tells me to leave for our children, but my heart tells me to stay for my parents.

The decision has been made that we will leave this May. We want to find land and get our first crop planted this spring so that we will have food and money for the rest of the year. I wish I was sure we are making the right decision.

I hear the first call of the *gök*. It came from the west. I'm relieved that the last time I hear this bird's prediction, it is a good omen. Now I know it is the direction we must take this year. West, across the ocean to America.

I never imagined us leaving this spot of earth, but we have no choice but to make our way to a new land. We won't have much to take with us, but reports of the promised land make us think we don't need to bring much along. This trip is for the survival of my children. Besides providing them with food and clothing, I want to give them the chance to prosper on land of their own. And the first step is to look for a new home across the sea.

Packing Tears

What should we take along, what can we do without? Where to pack it: into the big trunk, the sacks, or the baskets? I thought we owned few belongings until I started to plan for our voyage. Yes, we have few possessions, but everything we own has a purpose and should come with us!

I've been preparing, repairing, cleaning, baking for two weeks, just to get ready to pack. I've packed and repacked in my mind for weeks, and now that the task must be completed, I have done the same thing over and over! I've stashed the item I need, and then I have to dig through things to find it and pull it out. Farms tools to yarn skeins are strewn in piles around the room. Samuel is no help, and the children are in the way. I'm too upset at the moment to think. What I'd like to do is scream or cry.

We need our plates, bowls, cups, and eating utensils, but can't pack them until after our last meal in this house. We don't have many extra utensils, but they and the cooking pots and baking pans can go into the big trunk because we won't use them until we're done with our voyage. Samuel has carved many of my items, like the potato masher and spoons, out of wood. I will fit them in where I can.

I can take my butter mold, but the churn is too big to pack. Samuel promised to buy me new items as soon as we land in New York when I stood in the middle of the room, exasperated, trying to find places for things.

I need to pack food for our trip so that we don't have to buy it on our way to Göteborg. I know meals should be given to us on the ship, but I don't know if they will be enough, so maybe I should pack extra for that portion of the trip.

Rye was taken to the mill last week to be ground into flour so I could bake hard flat bread to take with us. Cheese wheels wrapped in new cloth. Meat and fish, salted and dried. A tub of salted butter. I need to make a sack for the last of the dried berries. Should I pack some honey along to quiet Emilia's sweet tooth and disposition? That would make a sticky mess if it spilled. Maybe we can just buy some sugar as a treat on the trip. I have a small carved bowl with a lid that would work to hold it.

Will we get porridge on the boat, or have a way to cook our own if we want to? I don't suppose there will be a cow on board the ship for milk. The children will have a hard time coping without that nourishment, but will only be for a week or two.

Towels will be needed for the trip. Will these things be furnished on the ship? What about a washbasin? Our pitcher for water? I must not forget soap!

All the clothing and bedding has been washed and mended. Material I made on the loom this winter has been cut and sewn into oversize clothes for the children. They are too big for them now, but the way Oscar is growing, they might fit him by the time we land on the shores of America.

The weather is still cold so that we need to wear our winter clothing. Will it be warm or cold on the ship? We've never been to the sea to know what the weather is like on the coast.

What will we wear in America? I've heard people say it is very hot there. Others have said it can be very cold. The place is so big that it has different kinds of weather. And so far we don't know where we will be homesteading yet. I'll take an empty sack to put our heavy coats in if we don't need them later.

Dresses, shirts, trousers, undergarments, petticoats, shawls, cloaks, aprons. Shoes and wooden clogs. Woolen socks and mittens. Where is Oscar's new hat he got from his *mormor* for Christmas?

I must prepare infant clothes also, because I'll be needing them before the year is out. I hope Emilia will be done with her linen diapers by then so they can be used when the baby arrives.

How do I wash clothes on the ship? Will there be a common washtub, hang lines to dry clothing from, good lye soap? The children soil their clothes so fast that things will have to be washed along the way.

Our bedding will be stuffed in heavy cloth sacks. The mattress tickings will be emptied of their straw stuffing and folded for use in our new house later this year. Do I dare take our goose-down pillows? They would take up so much room, but when would I have a chance to gather such a quantity of down and make new ones?

The quilts have been washed, and I can pull one out to use on the ship whenever I need to wrap a chilled child. I imagine they will be filthy by our arrival.

Our house is cramped with furniture that I wish we could take with us, but most of it belongs to Samuel's parents. They will continue living in the house, so the furniture stays. Tables, chairs, beds, rockers, and cupboards—how long before we have our own furnishings?

I have tried not to be sentimental, but I'm going to miss the loom and spinning wheel. Many hours of my married life have been connected to the rhythms of making linen and woolen material for our family. I will bring along the skeins of yarn I carded and spun last winter. It was too much work to leave behind. With my knitting needles, I'll try to get the yarn made into socks while we travel. I must remember to pick up my sewing basket, which I always leave sitting by my chair.

We need candles. What about the fireplace utensils we use to hang pots, to poke and stoke the fire? They were a wedding gift from Samuel's parents, so I'd like to take them. Could I use the braided rug in front of the fireplace to pad something else in order to justify taking it along? I made it last winter.

Samuel's initial attitude was "Don't worry about it! We'll buy new furniture and anything else we need when we get to America!" If he was in charge of the packing, I think he would only take a change of clothing and not bother with anything else.

But then tools starting moving from the shed to the living room where the big trunk lay open. A hammer, chisel, a packet of nails—in case the trunk needed repair. He couldn't leave the wood plane his grandfather gave him. He wanted something along that both their hands had touched. A small bag of rye so we can start the same variety of grain for the bread we are used to. A patch of leather and tools to repair shoes. I was expecting to see his favorite shovel in the house next. Samuel's pile started to rival my own in size.

We had planned to use an old trunk that was in the attic. But when it was emptied of its contents we decided it wasn't sturdy or big enough to travel all those miles. Samuel crafted a new trunk with our trip in mind. Besides making metal bands that encircle the middle in two places, his brother fashioned a lock built into the lid. With the key safe in Samuel's custody, our belongings will be locked from thievery when the box is out of our sight. On the front of the chest he carved his name and destination, "Samuel Fredrik Johansson, N. Amerika."

I also insisted we bring my *brudkista* along. My dowry was not large, Fader being a poor farmer and having two daughters marry at the same time, but I still had linens, our wedding cover, and clothing to bring to the marriage. The chest is not large enough to use as our main trunk, but it is big enough to put our clothes in that we will need for our trip.

We'll wear our Sunday parish clothes for getting on the boat. I want to look our best leaving the country. The children must not look like ragged urchins forced to leave their homeland. After we settle on the ship, we'll change into everyday clothes until we arrive at our destination.

Besides the necessities, we have few other things of value to bring along. My wedding gift from Samuel, a gold necklace, I'll wear under my clothing to keep it safe. I have sewn a money belt for Samuel to wear to keep our money hidden. He'll need to have some in his pocket along the way, but most of the money must be saved for our purchases when we start over on our new farm.

We have few books, but they can go in the *brudkista*: the *Bible*, psalmbook, a few books that Samuel and his siblings used to learn to read from. The *Handbook for America* that Samuel bought last fall when we started thinking about the trip must come along, although I think we have it all memorized by now. He read out loud from it almost every evening so we could familiarize ourselves with the climate and geography. It has put the children to sleep many nights. Maybe we'll use the same trick to put them to sleep on the boat.

What items could I put in the chest for the children to use to occupy their time? Even though they are young they helped with chores, explored the farm, or napped. They spent hours with their grandparents while Samuel and I worked outside in the fields. Oscar and Emilia don't have toys like rich children would have to play with. How am I going to manage to keep them entertained when they are confined on the trip?

The children are confused with the state of packing. Emily is too young to know anything except that there is stress and disorder in the house. Oscar asks "why" of everything.

"Why can't I take the cat with me?" "It needs to stay here to catch mice."

"Why isn't the farm *tomte* going with us?" "Because it needs to stay here to protect the farm."

"Why aren't Farfar and Farmor going with us?" "Because they want to stay in Sweden."

"Then why don't *we stay* too?"

I'll be at a loss myself without a home and farm to take care of. What am I going to do cooped up for weeks with no weaving to do, meals to cook, cows to milk? I'm used to working on the soil daily. Will I be terrified floating on the water with no way to touch dry land?

My envious brother Johan said I should think of this trip as an adventure on the high sea. No work to worry about for two weeks, just the chance to watch the world go by. With two young children to watch, I don't think that will be the case. I just hope we don't suffer from seasickness.

What is going to help me immensely is that my sister, Hedda, has decided to make the trip with us. Her year of employment is up this month, so instead of continuing with that household, she will journey to America and look for work. I'll still miss the rest of my family terribly, but having Hedda along has eased the panic that I was feeling at the thought of leaving them all.

My parents will be moving again, but this time to what I am leaving. They are moving to Kulla to replace Samuel's labor. My *fader* is twenty-five years younger than Samuel's and still has several years left before he can retire.

They will be moving into a tenant's house that stands adjacent to the farm compound. Johan and Sofia will be with them, but Mathilda has a job nearby. Where I stood in the garden, my *moder* will stand. My little sister, Sofia, will milk my cows and Fader will tend the rocky fields that Samuel and I worked to clear. Instead of me following in Fader's footsteps, he will be stepping into mine.

If only they would follow us to America. Then this packing wouldn't be so hard, and my belongings wouldn't be wet with my tears.

Leaving Home

One wagon full of belongings for the people leaving, another wagon full of the people leaving, and a third wagon of people along to see the first two wagons leave. It is such turmoil trying to get everything loaded this morning. Why didn't we do some of this last night?

Did we get everything out of the house? Anything else from the outbuildings? Where is the food basket? Is it on the bottom of the pile? Don't put the *brudkista* in yet! I can't find Emilia's shoes. I think Oscar might have put them in the chest. Do we have Hedda's trunk loaded? Is there still room for the Petterson's belongings when we stop to pick them up, or will we need to bring another wagon?

Samuel will drive the first wagon, Fader the second with us and the Pettersons. Johannes will drive the third wagon with everyone else who is going to the train station to see us off. But who will drive the first wagon back home? Oh, yes, my brother Johan will be along to do that.

We are fumbling in the dark hours before dawn to load our belongings for the first leg of our journey. It is a frosty morning, but we don't notice the cold as we trek between house and wagons. But I do know, now that the hour of departure is near, that I do not want the sun to rise on this May day.

No one, except the children, really slept last night.

I continued packing into the night. Clothes were folded into the wedding chest except for the ones laid out to be worn on our trip. The last of the household items were tucked in the big trunk. I had to pull out one pot because we could not get the trunk lid to shut. I saw Moder push something down the inside of the trunk, but she wouldn't tell me what is was or let me reach in to find out. She said to wait until we unpack the trunk.

I searched each room to see that everything of ours was packed. Trouble was, everything we have was mixed in with Samuel's parents' belongings.

And all the while I am thinking, this is the last time I look out this window, feel this door handle, smell the smoke from this fireplace. Several times I closed my eyes and used my other senses to memorize sensations and locations. The hairy side of the milk cow against my cheek as I milk her for the last time. The sixteen steps in the dark of the night from the door of the house to the door of the privy. The sad, wrinkled face of my worried father-in-law.

As the hours continued and the packing was done, we sat in the dark glow of the fire's dying embers and talked. Sad admissions, childhood tales recalled with laughter, strong advice from parents. Spoken hopes that this will be a prosperous adventure. Fader laughs, "Our children will write back bragging they own a thousand acres of American soil! I expect a new coat each year in my Christmas package since you'll have so much money, Lotta! And new boots from you, Hedda!"

This is the last chance to speak and listen to all our voices before the frenzy of the dawn. Years from now will I remember my Fader's occasional snore from this last night? Moder's advice mixed with words of love? Sister Sofia's crying? My own?

We must have looked like a group of gypsy vagabonds with our string of old farm wagons piled high with belongings and people as we turned onto the road to Mariannelund to meet our train. It was hard for me to look back at the Kulla homestead one last time, but I think it was worse for Samuel. During my childhood we moved many times, leaving one entrance yard but always pulling into another. But in Samuel's case, this is the only place he has ever lived.

I put an arm around his strong shoulders and gave him a slight squeeze of support. His gaze stayed straight ahead on the road and his hands on the reins, but there was a tremble in his face at my gesture. "Soon we'll have our own courtyard, Samuel, with a grand entrance to the house. On Sundays when we go to church you can pull up to the front door in a fancy carriage to collect your family and we'll ride to town in high style."

We stopped at the next Kulla farmstead, owned by Anders Magnusson, to pick up the Petterson family. Anders Peter Petersson is a relative of Samuel's family who came here from Lönneberga. He and his wife, Carolina, have three children, Augusta, Carl, and Emma, that are close in age to our children. Anders is a tailor and does all right—when people have money. He wants to start a business in America. I'm glad to have them as traveling companions.

Trunks, sacks, baskets piled high on the train platform and our belongings have not been added yet. We have tickets on an immigrant train heading straight for the port of Göteborg, so there are many other wagons besides ours unloading this morning.

We climb out of our seats, in awe of the busy confusion we are about to enter. Oscar shouts with delight at the sight of the train and darts toward it. Emilia squeals in panic because her *mormor's* grip has tightened as my *moder* senses our time together is almost gone.

Blurs of humanity. Young people in new clothes looking anxiously at the train they are about to board. Old people in peasant dress, waiting to see their children leave forever. Train porters trying to get people and baggage on board so the train can leave. Constant noise. The jingle of harness leather and creaking wood as another empty wagon pulls away from the platform. The puff puff of the train engine as it stokes up to leave. Laughter and cries of good-bys.

Smells of town and country mixed. Fresh manure dropped by a waiting horse. Coal smoke and ash filtering down from the smokestack. Fresh baked bread from dozens of food baskets. It is starting to drizzle, and people worry about getting their baggage wet and keeping bundled children from catching cold before they start the journey. Someone snickers, "Now when we're leaving the farm, it decides to rain!"

Our senses are alert to danger, excitement, and sadness. Everyone is looking forward but also dreading the moment of departure as they prepare to leave home forever.

"Watch out for the falling trunk!"

"Look how many cars this train has, Mamma! Which one do we get to ride in?"

"Keep your money safe in that pouch I made you, Daughter. And don't speak to strangers!"

"What needs to stay with us, Charlotta? Is everything marked with our name? Don't let Oscar get too close to the tracks!" Samuel, red-faced with anxiety, is barking questions and orders at me until his father steps in to help. "It is done, Samuel. You have made the right choice for your family. God speed, Son."

Long hugs, handshakes, kisses, and wet faces. We huddle together in little groups beside the train. The whistle is blowing and half the travelers have not boarded the train to find their seats.

One last gaze into Fader's eyes as we both break down and hug again. My bashful brother's handshake. Mathilda's surprising vow to follow us to America soon, and Moder's shocked look as she hears she might lose another child.

Bulky luggage, dawdling children, a crowded aisle. We're overloaded trying to get us, our baskets, and our children to our seats. "Keep going, Oscar! Where is Hedda? Is there room for her here or—no, she has taken a seat with someone else she knows. I think Pettersons must be in another car, because I don't see them. I hope everything and everyone in our party is on this train!"

We get settled, then search through the rain-stained window for our family, still standing outside in the mass of people. Just as I see my parents, the train jerks forward. Emilia slips from my lap and I tear my gaze away from them to grab my child. When I look back out the window, they are gone.

The children finally settle down. The rocking motion of the train has made them drowsy. Before the day is over they will be awake, bored, and tired of being confined to one place. The rocking makes me slightly queasy. I'm exhausted but can't seem to sleep myself. Staring out the window, I view the landscape that we have already passed because my seat faces the back of the car. I see what we are leaving and will never see again.

We crossed over nine Swedish miles of country on the first leg of our trip. At first the scenery was familiar, but it changed as we gained distance. I had never before been outside of our county, so this was the first and last time I would see Sweden. Much of the landscape was the same as ours in Pelarne—hints of green, but not the lush of fresh grass we should be seeing by now. Stands of forests opened up into meadows and closed back again.

Southern portion of Sweden, circa 1800s

Small lakes had low shorelines because of the lack of water. Ancient manors and fortresses of our Viking ancestors flew by. Blurs of homesteads, old barns with thatched roofs, dark red farmhouses, a small herd of cows with new calves. Piles of rocks in the fields. A farmer looking up from his work to watch the train go by. What is he thinking as he sees this train of emigrants?

We saw churches of ancient stone built centuries ago or newer wooden structures. We noticed the style of the steeple change from one province of Sweden to another as we traveled across the country. A graveyard surrounds each church like a protective shield. Underneath the tombstones lie ancestors we will never visit again. It is customary for the living to take care of the dead's spot of earth. Who will take care of the graves if all the young people leave Sweden?

As we pass churches I wonder if people had problems getting their transfer papers to leave the congregation. Unfortunately, many pastors are trying to discourage their congregations from moving to America. The church has a strong rein on its people. It is not a sheltered haven anymore for lost souls. It is a dictatorship and another reason for some to flee.

Villages that we never knew existed passed before our sight. We stopped briefly at Eksjö and Nässjö to pick up passengers. You could tell the ones who were leaving their homes for good. Family and friends clung to these people until the last call for departure. Waves and tears good-by, then forlorn parents left standing on the platform. Just like mine.

How many people had left home and traveled this same track, wondering the same thoughts? All wondering if we could have done something different in order to stay, and if we will ever travel back again if our fortunes turn around.

We had a long stop at Jonköping, on the shore of Lake Vättern. The train followed the water's edge before we pulled into the depot, so we could see the width of the lake. We had traveled out of the rain and now had clear sunshine. I don't know how far north the water went because we couldn't see land on the other end. I have never seen a body of water so big and couldn't help wondering what the ocean will look like. No trees, land, or hills in the distance. Only water in all directions. The thought makes me uneasy.

Samuel ventured off the train during our stopover to stretch his legs and to check on the Pettersons. I would have liked to have done the same, but I had sleeping children and baggage piled around me. At least fresh air came in, because the doors were opened up. The car had gotten warm and stuffy with all the people packed in it.

Hedda came back to me after the crowd in the aisle thinned out. She found that several other young people we know are also on this train bound for Göteborg. Talking to them, she is excited about the venture and hasn't dwelt on the past, as I have. So-and-so is going to a relative's home in Illinois. Someone else has a job waiting for them in the south, because that employer has paid his passage to America. Another plans to go far west to the California gold mines to get rich fast so he can come back to Sweden.

I just sat and listened to her excited talk. My mind kept drifting back to the train depot at Mariannelund.

We traveled another twelve Swedish miles with two more brief stops before pulling into the port of Göteborg this evening. The car had turned into quiet silence except for the crying of an occasional restless baby. Conversations all but ceased among the weary passengers. Everyone is tired from the day's journey, and thinking about the magnitude of what they have set into motion by getting on and now off this train.

Twilight shimmers off the sea's horizon as we gaze out at our final stop. The central station is a few blocks away from the water, but we can still see tall gray sails of boats gently swaying above the buildings that must line the pier. People are milling up and down the streets, ignoring our emigrant train. I imagine these trains have become so common that the citizens don't pay any attention to them. However, few men searching into our windows look like they are waiting for this train to arrive.

I hope the ship's agent is here to meet us so we know where to go next. We are at the mercy of others to get us across the sea.

Tonight this exhausted trainload of people will be ushered to a hotel to spend the night. I image our accommodations will be sparse, but we're ready to sleep anywhere, on anything that isn't moving. I feel like I might rock all night like this car, but I think sleep will find me quickly. I'm exhausted from today's journey, yesterday's packing, and last month's decision.

Samuel is still in a somber mood. He has talked politely to other people, but has kept quiet most of the day while sitting with us. I can tell he is lost in thought, thinking about the home and family we left behind this morning. His shadowed eyes reveal that he is still going over the same questions. "Can the children and Charlotta stand the rigors of the journey? Can we find land in America? How will I make a living if we can't? How much do things cost in America? Do we have enough money stashed in my money belt? What will happen to us if the belt is lost or stolen? Did we make the right decision to leave?"

I can't help him with these questions, because I don't know the answers either. We must trust that our faith gave us the right answer and continue our trip tomorrow. We have completed the first leg of our journey to Göteborg, a seaport since the 1600s. Swedes sailed to America during that century from here, so we're just following their sails.

If they could do it, so can we.

The First Step

Last night was the first time I have ever slept in a bed that was not in a house, and with people I did not know. Hedda, the children, and I slept in one bed. Carolina and her three slept in the bed beside us. Samuel was with Anders and some strange man in another. A fourth bed held the stranger's wife and family. Our bed was lumpy and uncomfortable, but we all slept because we were tired.

Something we'll have to get used to on this trip is the absence of privacy from other passengers. We shared the hotel room with two other families last night, making it hard to change clothes or clean ourselves. To change a baby's diaper in company is one thing; to undress in front of a stranger is something else. I'm sure Hedda and I will become adept at ensuring our privacy.

We had a breakfast of porridge, rye bread, and milk in the dining room of the hotel this morning. After eating three meals out of a basket yesterday, the children were ready for a real meal. I keep thinking that tomorrow morning we'll eat our last breakfast in Sweden.

The men left early this morning to find the ship agent's office on the *Sillgata* to pick up our reserved boarding tickets and to make sure our baggage is transferred. They were informed that there would be a long line, because hundreds of people will be doing the same thing. The ship does not sail for England until tomorrow evening, but we want to be sure to get our tickets for the ship.

We explored Göteborg and were overwhelmed by the sights. We stared up at the massive churches, peered into brick shops lined on cobblestone streets, and marveled at the trappings of city life. We felt like farm peasants walking down the streets of a foreign country. The streets seemed to go on and on. Could a person walk from one end of the town to the other in a day? Samuel kept saying, "What must New York City be like? Or Chicago? Cities are supposed to be gigantic in America!"

But the pull was down to the sea. This is where we spent most of the day as we waited to board our ship. The salt air, cold wind, and noise from the water's edge overwhelmed our senses. So much to see and absorb. The harbor was so full of boats that we wondered how they maneuvered in and out to the docks. Bobbing little boats, like the ones we used to row on the lake west of Pelarne, to gigantic ships with over thirty sails. A steam liner with two decks. Can you see the name on its side? That's the ship from the Wilson line that we will get on in a few hours!

Ropes, nets, and cargo was piled on wooden piers that jutted out over the water. There was the smell of fish, bird droppings, wet wood. Sky blue and sun yellow flags snapped in the brisk wind, and sailors called out orders in languages we don't understand. Activity is everywhere as boats are loaded with Swedish timber, barrels marked "Salted Herring," and emigrants' belongings. Seaman are unloading ships flying flags from England and other countries.

Oscar starts his "What's that?" questioning, and for the most part I'm wondering the same things.

Screaming gulls fly overhead, making circles in the air, then swooping into the ocean to snatch a fish from the waters. The noisy birds are everywhere: standing on the pier, on a ship's railing, flapping from place to place. They are so at ease here that they hardly move out of one's way when we walk along the dock.

"Get on! Get on the boat!" Samuel calls to me above the din of the gulls and dock loaders. I did not want to be the first to get on the ship, but I have no choice. I hold my breath as I step onto the gangplank. It's one thing to look at the ship from a distance and another to be walking onto it by a long stretch of movable boards high above the dark water. Emily's legs are scissored around my waist, and her little arms encircle my neck. Her face is buried in my shoulder so that she doesn't see down. Oscar is clutching the hem of my dress with one hand and Hedda's with the other. Samuel brings up the rear, his arms laden with the possessions we must keep with us.

I hesitantly make my way up the walk, then freeze as a gull lands on the gangplank a yard ahead of me. Any movement makes me feel like I'm going to lose my balance and cause us all to topple into the water below. My steps are my family's destiny. Another step, the bird flies off, and we're safely on the ship. Only then do I realize I am no longer touching Swedish soil.

The ship slides slightly up and down in the water, but the motion is not as bad as I thought it would be. Rows of benches line enclosed big rooms and the decks to hold the passengers as we make the crossing to England. The hard seats are soon crowded as people place their belongings on them. There is not much space to stretch out and sleep, but it is only a short trip to England. We are in the steerage and cannot occupy the expensive cabins on the top deck.

We marked a section of bench space for us with our belongings, but we have a few hours to wait before we leave. So we stand at the rail, looking back at other people still boarding, back at the harbor's activities, back at Sweden. Looking from this higher angle we see more of the harbor, which stretches for miles in either direction.

To the northwest we can see the mouth of the Göta River, which flows into the Cattegat. There on its bank towers the stronghold of Bohus Castle. Built by Norway centuries ago to guard the entrance to its ancient border, it has been in Sweden's possession for the last two hundred years. From its point one can sail up the river, through the manmade Göta Canal and Sweden's natural lakes, all the way across Sweden to Stockholm. Produce from Sweden's interior, timber and iron ore, are transported down the lakes to the sea. The idea for the canal was in existence three hundred years ago, but the canal itself was completed only about forty years ago.

The harbor takes on a yellow glow as the sun starts to slide toward the horizon. The gangplank is detached from the dock and pulled into our ship. My heart races because there is no way to get off this boat now. We're on our way to America and there is no turning back.

Orders are given, whistles blown, and the huge anchor on its gigantic iron chain is winched up out of the water by a rally of seaman. The next wave that hits the ship gently rocks it sideways. There is a definite feeling of no longer being connected to anything. We are now at the sea's mercy.

The sun sets as the ship steers out into the Cattegat. I want to stand on deck as long as we can see land. The large ships we were anchored by grow smaller and smaller. The church steeple that rose above the city is fading in the distance. Ships that left before and after us dot the horizons in various sizes, depending on how fast they are moving through the water. The granite shoreline turns a bright red-brown as the sun leaves the rocks. And then I have to squint to see the shoreline of Sweden in the remaining light.

Silence, then muffled sobs among the crowd. Tears running down both men's and women's cheeks. Someone starts to sing the Swedish anthem. Another is offering a prayer for safety on the voyage. I can no longer see the country where I was born. And I doubt I'll ever see it again.

The trip to Hull, England, took two days. Most of the time we sat huddled on the benches, trying to sleep. We occasionally went back to the deck for fresh air, but the cold wind soon blew us back in. When we rounded the tip of Denmark and entered the North Sea, the high waves made us seasick until we sailed into calmer water. I did not bother to unpack the food basket the first morning, because the food would have been wasted. We would not have been able to keep it in our stomachs. I do not know if I suffered from seasickness or morning sickness, but I was miserable at times.

People milled around the ship both day and night, talking, pacing, staring out to sea. A few musical instruments were unpacked to accompany singing. Games were played, books read, someone practiced their English. Everyone was waiting. These first two days were not bad, but what about the long trip from England to America?

One of us always had a hold of Emilia for fear she would toddle away and topple between the side rails into the sea. Oscar was almost as big a worry as he grew more confident of his sea legs. To the children on the ship, this is just a trip. They ask, "When will we go home again?" There is no way to make them comprehend that we are moving to another country, or that we are doing it for them.

Slowly the coast of England grew from a tiny dot to large cliffs of green. The sea vessel grew calm as we sailed up the River Humber. More boats joined us as we sailed into the harbor of Hull. It grew dark before we are allowed to depart from this ship. Even though we walked onto a different country's soil tonight, it feels good to have solid earth beneath us again.

This time we knew what to expect. Emigrant agents met us at the dock, escorted us to a hotel, and we spent another night crowded in too few beds. The only difference was we could not read the street signs or understand the English language. Now we were totally dependent on the agent's help.

At midmorning we boarded the train for Liverpool, the harbor port on the west side of England. This time I got a seat so I could view the scenery as we met it. The few hours it takes the train to cut across the country saves us the time and expense of sailing all the way around the island of Britain.

England's beautiful countryside rolled endlessly as far as we could see. Samuel commented on the difference between their sparse clumps of trees as compared to our thick forests. The fields were cut into little patchworks of plantings and meadows. Of course the farmers in our group were trying to figure of what had been planted so far this spring. Being farther south, England's spring comes earlier than Sweden's.

It was noticeably warmer in England, and vegetation was greener than what we had left three days ago. The agent said we were lucky that it wasn't raining and cloudy today, the usual weather.

Large herds of sheep, both shorn and unshorn of their winter wool, dotted the slopes. Cows and pigs were different kinds than the ones we tended. So much was the same, but yet there were subtle differences. English farmhouses were shaped differently than Sweden's. More stone is used in England, whereas Sweden has plenty of timber for buildings. England's castles and churches look centuries old, like Sweden's. Some were in ruins, but others were still in use. People dressed differently.

We went through villages without stopping unless we needed to pick up fuel and water for the train. Housing in the smaller towns consisted of squat one-story row houses made of brick and thatch. The exception was Manchester, which was a much larger town and had more commerce and larger houses.

The air changed the closer we got to Liverpool. There was a distinct smell, causing everyone to wonder who it was coming from until we realized it was coming from outside. The closer we got to the city, the more gray and hazy the air became. Smoke-stacks polluted the air with smoke from the town's factories. We went through areas of slums, rows of run-down houses stacked on top of one another. It seemed we traveled for miles within the city limits before we reached the train depot.

From our car window we watched dozens of dirty street children begging money from anyone who walked by. If a police-

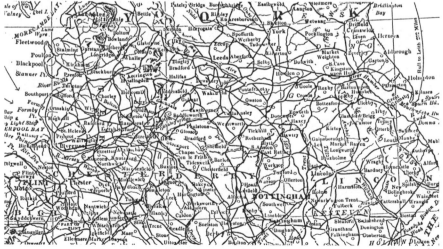

Northern section of England, circa 1800s

man came into view, the urchins scattered down the alleys. Even though they were pestering people, my heart went out to them. Where were their parents? Why were they reduced to begging? But it was getting to be the same sad case in parts of famished Sweden. Parents were too proud to ask for help, so they sent their children out looking for food.

Seeing the dirty side of Liverpool made us leery of getting off the train and to our hotel safely. I hardly slept last night for fear of our family's health in the dilapidated hotel we had to stay in. We slept in our street clothes because of the dirty sheets on the bed. We itched all night from the bed bugs, listened to mice scurry across the floor, and stepped on huge cockroaches as they ran from the morning candlelight. I also worried about our possessions that were still sitting in the baggage car of the train we departed. My only comfort was that our heavy trunk was locked and Samuel had the key.

This morning we went down to the Princes Dock bright and early, just to get out of our hotel room. The men reluctantly left our group of women and children to check on the transfer of our luggage. I felt like we mothers were a ring of cows, protecting our calves from the wolves.

The activity around us was similar to Göteborg. The Liverpool docks were crowded with packs of people. We recognized

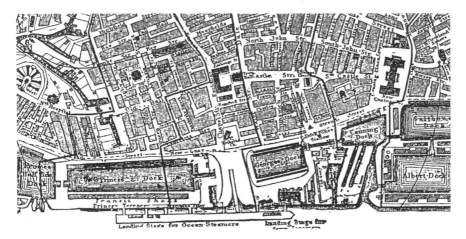

Liverpool Harbor, circa 1800s

33

Norwegians and Germans because their language is similar to ours. Even if we don't hear the English speak, we know their nationality because of their dress and their actions. Another giveaway is that their men are usually shorter than Swedish men. I was separated from Samuel this morning while we were walking down the street. Local people were on their way to work and we were caught in the commotion. I looked back to find him, and he towered a head and a half above everyone else.

There were several ships from different lines docked in the harbor, so people were looking for certain piers and ship lines. We saw ships from the Anchor, Cunard, Inman, and White Star lines. Some were magnificent specimens of steel and paint. Others didn't look seaworthy.

Boats were also sailing into Liverpool from America. The people disembarking from a ship we watched were well dressed. Women in tailored coats wore fancy hats instead of shawls and head scarves. Most men sported silk top hats. They unloaded manufactured trunks instead of homemade chests from the cargo. I couldn't help but dream that someday it might be us traveling back to Sweden in the best clothes money could by.

But first we have to get there and make our fortune.

The ship we've boarded is a city by itself. We got lost just trying to find our way to quarters. We're on the ship's lowest level. Steerage class isn't the most comfortable, but we can count the days until we will be off the ship.

People holding steerage tickets were boarded first because the ship loaded from the bottom up. First class passengers on the top deck leisurely strolled on last. Because we are in steerage, we will not be allowed past our deck floor for the duration of the trip.

We found out that women and men are separated in different sections of this ship, so I'll have the children with me. I wish Samuel was in our room to help with the children, but Hedda will be with me instead. There are so many single people on board, that they don't want to use a whole room for a family.

We are in a little stuffy cabin without a window for air or scenery. By the time everyone added their baggage there was barely room to walk to the bunks that line the walls. Thin mattresses of straw are the only bedding provided, but I have blankets along.

It is crowded with so many people on board. And we're scheduled to stop in Ireland to pick up more passengers. There are supposed to be about one thousand passengers and over one hundred shipmates when we head into the Atlantic Ocean. That is more than double the people we had on the ship from Sweden to England.

The ship is three stories high with iron fences and promenades around each deck. A shipmate told us it is four hundred feet in length from stern to bow. On each level there is a large salon for sitting and meals. Passenger cabins line long hallways running the entire length of the ship.

At least steamships designed for carrying passengers have greatly improved in the last few decades. We will make the trip within two weeks, whereas it took two to four months to sail ships across the Atlantic a few decades ago. Those boats would sit in one spot for days if the wind died down because it was the only power available to move the ship.

Loading took hours, so we have had time to settle in and go back on deck for departure. Now the whistles are blowing and we are about to leave. The cargo has been loaded and there are just a few latecomers rushing to jump on board.

One family down by the gangplank catches my eye. They were in line in front of us when we were getting on the ship earlier in the day. When we boarded, there was a Swedish doctor standing by the gangplank watching people as they walked by. He pulled aside anyone who looked sick. They don't want a contagious disease to spread among the passengers or be taken to America. This family, the one still on the dock, was detained because the husband was carrying a half-grown boy. The doctor questioned the parents and examined the child. Yes, the parents admitted he had been sick, but they didn't know what was wrong with him. They hoped the sea air would cure him. We only caught part of their conversation before walking on, but I overheard the doctor say that the boy had a high fever.

Now the gangplank is being pulled away from the pier, and the husband is still pleading with the doctor to let his family on.

What is the family going to do now? I'm sure they traveled quite a distance to get this far, but now they aren't being allowed on. Do they have enough money to stay in a hotel until the child is better? To buy medicine? Will they be able to exchange their tickets for another ship's?

I'll always wonder what happened to that family. And remember the panic I'd be feeling if that was me stranded on the dock watching my ship leave.

Route to North America, circa 1800s

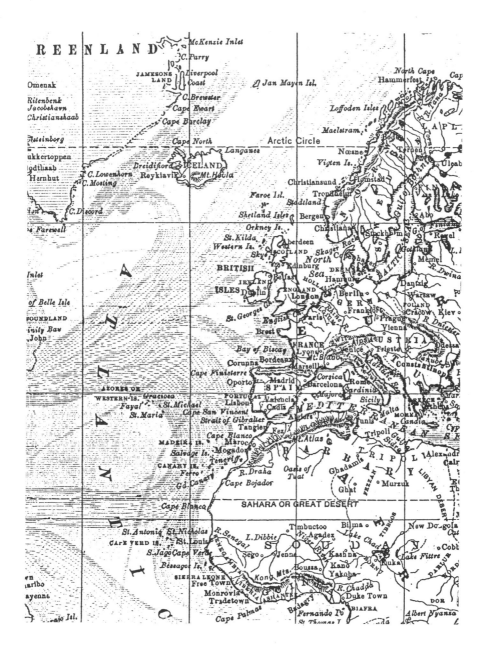

Sailing the Atlantic

We left the port sailing into a wall of fog. We didn't stay at the deck rail long because there was nothing to see once we were a short distance from the harbor. No land to watch fade in the distance, only a solid cloud that seemed to suspend the boat in midair. I felt bad for the English emigrants. They did not have the pleasure of seeing their country at a distance like we did.

The other reason most people left the decks was to get away from the noise. Besides the clanging of bells and roar of the steam engines, the foghorn was blowing every few seconds to warn other boats of our location. We could hear horns from other boats echoing off one another, and we couldn't tell which direction they were coming from. We just hoped there were no collisions in this thick fog.

How people spent their days on board depended on the weather. People looked forward to the three meals a day unless the weather was bad. They were served on long tables in the big room on our level. Large pots of food were set out, then people dipped their own bowls in to get their portions. I tried to be toward the front of the line when the food came. I cringed every time I saw a dirty person dip a filthy bowl into the common pot.

The food has rarely varied the whole trip. The usual fare is a watery fish soup, black bread, and boiled potatoes. The children have missed their milk or porridge. We supplemented the meal with our own cheese while it lasted.

If the water was rough the ship would roll sideways, or rise up and then plunge down with the waves. It didn't have a rhythm, as it would have on the calm sea, and people and objects were thrown off balance. Meals were delayed because it was impossible to keep the food from sliding off the tables. We weren't allowed outside during these times because the waves sprayed onto the deck and a person could be washed over the railing with the force of the wind and water. One stormy night I bruised my shoulder when I was thrown against the wall when trying to walk down the hall to the toilet.

When it was bad people stayed in their quarters, usually seasick in bed. The smell from the vomit buckets made everyone queasy. Rooms were cleaned by the people staying in them, so there were a few days when the buckets weren't emptied when we had the storm. I missed the bucket once myself.

The children seemed to fare the best with the seasickness. Oscar and Emilia slept through the worst of the storms. They just rolled in the bunk with the waves.

We witnessed one death during the voyage. I don't know if the elderly man's death was caused by sickness or old age. We happened to sit by him one night for supper and he told us where he was from and headed to. He pulled out well-read letters from his coat pocket to share his excitement with us. His son had a prosperous farm in America and had sent him a ticket to come see it. The gentleman was happy about the trip. His entire life was spent trying to scratch a living out of a few acres of rocky soil. He wanted to see and feel this rich earth in America that yielded such big harvests.

He was a widower, living with a daughter's family. Failing in health and no longer able to work, he felt his time in life was almost over. I felt so sorry for him. He wanted to see his son's accomplishments with his own eyes before he died, but he didn't live long enough. The captain held a funeral on the deck for the man. The body was sewn into a canvas bag to which weights had been added. It lay on a plank across two sawhorses, with the foot end of the plank resting on top of the ship railing.

A few words were said and a Swedish hymn was sung by those who gathered around. Before the body was dropped overboard the captain sprinkled three handfuls of soil across the body. It was to represent the traditional shovels of earth we Swedish throw into the grave at burial. A bushel basket of Swedish soil was kept on board for that purpose. At the time I wished one handful of earth could have come from America for the old man. He wanted so much to touch his son's soil.

The ship bell tolled once for the dead, and then the body was dropped overboard to sink to the sea's floor.

When the weather was fair people stayed on deck except to sleep and eat. Fresh air was the preferred choice of anyone who was upright. Time was passed talking, or staring out at the sea.

Whether in the air or in the sea, there were birds and fish to watch for. The birds were thick around the harbors but became more scarce as we got further into the voyage. It was a real treat to see a bird land on the ship. People would throw stale bread crumbs its way to make it stay a while. We wondered what kind it was, and where had come from. How many miles had it flown since it last touched land? Out here on the sea we longed for some living thing that belonged to the ground, even if it had only touched the top of a tree.

People fished off the sides of the ship, and the catches were added to the soup of the day. Cod was the usual catch, but sometimes a shipmate had to identify strange specimens. Time was spent watching playful dolphins dive in and out of the water alongside the ship. They would come from nowhere, follow us for minutes or hours, then leave again. We even saw some whales at a distance. The wind and water brought us things to marvel at, but they always disappeared as fast as they same.

Men stood in groups along the rails comparing notes of what they had heard about the country we were heading toward. Several had handbooks that described areas of America. "Where is the best place to find land?" "What does your book say about the weather in Colorado? Is it safe to travel west with all the Indian stories we're heard about?" "Where are you going to settle?" "Are you going on to the established Swedish settlements in Illinois or Minnesota?" "Has anyone read the newspaper articles about the railroad land for sale in Kansas?"

Ideas and questions were discussed, minds changed, worries brought out in the open. "Where and when will we find a new home?" "Can I find a job right away?" "Were the advertisers telling the truth about free land available to anyone?" Our destiny was plotted and rewritten several times over the course of our voyage.

People practiced American phrases out loud. They studied their translation books, said the phrase in Swedish, then English, trying to comprehend the strange sounds.

"*God morgon.* Good morning."

"*Kan ni hjälpa mig?* Can you help me, please?"

"*Var ligger järnvägsstationen?* Where is the railway station, please?"

"*Tack så mycket.* Thank you very much."

Those of us with young children had a different routine. Healthy or sick, children had to be watched, cleaned, and rocked to sleep. My daily washing of Emilia's soiled linens decorated a line across our room during the whole trip. Fathers might occasionally check their children while they were on deck, but most of the looking-after fell to the mothers. When we were all on deck I'd read to the children or just watch them play. There were many families on board, but over half the passengers were unmarried.

Sometimes I'd just stare into the horizon, lost in thought. What were our parents doing at this moment? Is Fader making progress with the field north of the house? Samuel and I started clearing the rocks from that plot last fall. Has it rained yet? Will they have food for winter?

The evening stars found the young single people singing and dancing on the deck until the wee hours of the morning. For the servants that had worked on someone else's farm, this idle time was heaven. Most had left home at an early age and never had a holiday, except for possibly one week a year when they went back to visit parents (who usually put them to work). Now they had a few weeks to enjoy doing nothing, and most of them did just that. Hedda joined in some nights, dancing with whoever asked her.

It might be a Swedish song, then someone else came up with an Irish jig. People from different countries stayed separate, except when there was dancing and music. Even though there might be different tunes and words, everyone could enjoy the music.

The first class passengers were entertainment for all ages. They often watched us from their higher deck. Shouting matches happened now and then, but most of it was good natured. Sometimes they would drop coins or food down to the lower deck. Oscar caught an American penny one day. He was as proud that he caught it as he was of the coin. Their meals featured a variety of fresh fruit that we couldn't believe they would throw away instead of eating. When something like that started dropping down, there was a mad scramble to catch it.

But one morning the attention on all the decks changed to our destination in one quick second. A shout of "Land!" was all it took for everyone to rush to the railing. America had been sighted! It is barely visible, but there is a thin wisp of a coastline in the distance. Eyes are glued to the distance while the shoreline slowly enlarges.

We crossed three thousand miles of water since leaving Liverpool ten days ago. During this suspension of time I've thought about what we left behind and what lay ahead for us. Now the future is growing in the horizon.

Am I ready for the challenge?

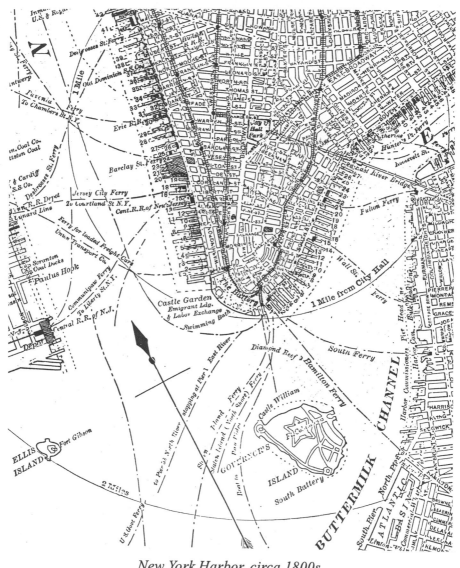

New York Harbor, circa 1800s

Ready to Depart

"There it is! America! We're here!! Look, Look!"

People spill out onto the decks, shoving forward to the rail, craning their necks to stare at the sight coming into view. "We made it!" There is pointing, laughing, fervent prayers. Bursting into tears, we realize we are sailing into American waters. Fathers lift their small children up so they can see. We all want to stare at our dream—and our new home.

At first it was a hazy view as we traveled parallel to the coast of New York. Then we left the open sea and traveled up the narrows of New York Bay. Land grew closer and closer until we could see the shoreline clearly.

It took time to navigate up the harbor. Hundreds of boats of all kinds maneuvered in a waterway that was as busy as a city street. There were tugboats, fishing boats, small sailing boats clipping through the waters. I counted a dozen steamers meeting and then passing us on their way out to sea. From their mastheads waved colorful flags from different countries. I'll bet there were more than that number following us into the harbor to deposit emigrants onto the shore.

New York City sits on a group of large islands that are connected by bridges or ferries. We passed two small islands in the harbor. We were told they were Ellis Island and the much bigger Governor's Island. Both had been as forts in earlier wars.

We went another English mile before docking near a tip of land that stuck out in the harbor. From this point of the bay, ships veering left would continue up the Hudson River or to the right for the East River.

Next came the rush to depart. Everyone dashed back to their quarters to gather up their belongings. For the single people with only a satchel or two it wasn't hard to get organized and back on deck. I thought I was ready, but there were still things to do. Blankets were folded and put away this morning, but Emilia had rummaged around the sack to pull out her favorite again. Half-dry diapers still hung on a line in the room. We needed to check under the bunks for things that might have rolled underneath. Food was stuffed back in the basket. Everything fit in our luggage a week ago, but it doesn't seem to now that I'm in a hurry.

The wedding chest had to be packed and repacked again because I also needed to change clothes. I didn't think it mattered what we wore this morning because we're still traveling, but Samuel suggested we wear our best clothes on our arrival. He didn't want us to look like a poor peasant family getting off the boat.

Our ship's deck is covered with anxious people ready to depart. Groups are clustered together for fear of separation. Everyone's arms are loaded down with sacks, baskets, and children. And we all just stand here waiting to get off this moving boat and onto solid land again.

Our destination is the Castle Garden Emigrant Center located on the Battery of Manhattan Island. We'll have to wait, though, because the waterfront is crowded and there are a number of ships waiting for a mooring in front of us.

Hours later the ship is anchored and we're allowed off. Slowly the crowd dwindles as groups of passengers are boarded onto ferries to be taken to the dock. It has become a waiting game. The ferry loads up, goes to shore, unloads, comes back to our ship for another load, and goes back to the dock again.

And then it's our turn.

"Keep together. Oscar, hold my hand!" The crush of people push us down the gangplank onto the bobbing ferry. Samuel comments that he feels like an animal being prodded into a wagon to go to market. Someone behind us replies that it is more like too many Swedish salted herrings stuffed in an old wooden barrel. I just hope we don't sink and drown this close to our destination.

After a short ride we're free to touch the soles of our shoes to land again. I blink back tears to stare at the American flag flying on top of the immigration center. I sway into Samuel. The ground feels solid, yet it moves like the rhythm of the ship. Several people drop on their knees to kiss the ground and say a prayer of thanks. They had waited so long to get away from their troubles that they are overwhelmed to be finally in the promised land.

Before we are free to travel to our destination, we must pass this country's inspection.

As our line slowly moved ahead, we had time to look at the building. The inside space is divided into medical examination rooms, offices, information stands, and a large area in the middle with benches.

We found out that Castle Garden, formally known as Fort Clinton, was part of the strategic defense of the harbor during the War of 1812. The enormous octagonal-shaped fort of red sandstone was built on artificial landfill on the bay's edge. After the war, a roof was put on the structure to serve as a reception center, resort, and restaurant. The hall seated six thousand people, becoming the largest one in the country. Jenny Lind, the Swedish Nightingale, gave her first American concert here in 1850. But the resort did not succeed financially, so it became New York's first immigration center in 1855.

The din of voices is overwhelming. The babble of different languages mix in with shouts, crying, laughter, and orders. Everyone is trying to talk above the drone of the crowd.

Children (and adults) are tired of standing in line; they're hungry or need the toilet. We still have on our coats, and it is hot and stuffy in here. We are also nervous because the inspection is coming up. While waiting, we hear stories of sick people being sent back to their countries. A doctor examines everyone while they are in line. If closer inspection is needed, a person is ushered into a private room. The weak and sick are quarantined in the infirmary. Anything serious could cause deportation.

What happens if a child is ill? Someone said a child of ten or older can be sent back alone. What if the child is younger? In most cases the parents wouldn't have the money to buy return passage for the family. Another person said sometimes the inspectors can be bribed to let sick children pass. What would we do in that situation?

We move in front of a man standing beside a high stand that holds medical instruments. One by one, he examines our eyes, throats, thumps our chests, looks for signs of disease or disability. Emilia jerks away and cries when the doctor tries to check her. A quiet word in the child's ear of "a taste of sugar later if you talk to the nice doctor" got us past our first inspection.

Next came the collection and inspection of our luggage. We identified our big trunk and opened sacks and baskets, through which the inspector searched quickly. I'm not sure what they are looking for, because we didn't have room for anything but our own possessions.

Now it is our turn to stand in front of the registration clerk. This one doesn't even look up at Samuel. He dips his pen in the inkwell, poises it over the page of the register, and starts to fire his list of questions in English. When there is no answer from the tall Swede he looks up, assesses the identity of the foreigner, and asks his questions again in halting Swedish.

"Name?"

"Samuel Fredrik Johansson."

As he is writing, he says "Samuel F. Johnson."

"No! Johansson, not Jonsson!"

"Johnson is the American version of your last name."

"Oh. Yes, sir."

"Wife's name?"

"Christina Charlotta Samuelsdotter."

"Christina Johnson."

"She goes by Charlotta Samuelsdotter."

"Wives go by their husband's last name in America. 'Charlotta Johnson'."

"Oh. Yes, sir."

"Children?"

"Carl Johan Oscar Samuelsson and Emilia Christina Samuelsdotter."

"And they go by what name?"

"Oscar and Emilia."

"They'll be registered as 'Oscar and Emily Johnson.' Your occupation?"

"Farmer."

"How will you earn your living?"

"I'm going to own a big farm."

"Hum. Homesteading."

"How much money do you have on you?"

"It is still in *riksdaler*. I haven't exchanged it yet so I don't know what it is worth in American money."

"Limited funds."

"Ever been convicted of a crime?"

"What?! No, sir."

"You all have the checkmark from the doctor? Good. Has any of your family ever had any contagious diseases?"

"Not that I know of."

"Is anyone meeting you here to help you?"

"No, we're on our own."

"Check outside when you leave the building. There usually are Swedish clergymen there to help the Scandinavians. What is your final destination?"

"Andover, Illinois."

With the stroke of a pen this man has changed our names and recorded us as poor farmers heading west. I hope to remedy the latter soon.

"Did he give you the right amount?"

"I have no idea."

We moved away from the money exchange window and stared at the wad of bills and coins cupped in Samuel's hands. He had emptied his money belt of the Swedish currency he had carefully protected on our trip and gave it to the man to exchange. Our life savings was now coverted to American money. Not only do we need it to get to Illinois, but it has to last until we get our farm established.

"May I help you? Where are you heading next?"
A man in a preacher's collar speaking Swedish!
"We need to get to Illinois."
"Let's go to the train room and see about your tickets. It will cost about twenty-six dollars to get your family there. Do you have enough money?"

The Swedish pastor and his volunteers checked the center every day to help the Scandinavians that had arrived on the day's ships. Part of their mission work was to get these confused souls through customs and on their way to their new lives. People needing help to exchange money, track down lost luggage, get food for their continuing journey are taken under his wing. A baby born at sea needs baptizing. A young one has been orphaned and needs a new home. A child is sick and her parents need a translator. They don't understand why they are being detained and separated. Maybe intervention can save the child from being deported.

Another family spent their last dollar to get on the ship. Now they have no money for food or board. The pastor finds a poorhouse to shelter them until the father finds a job. The pastor helps the new arrivals write letters back to relatives to announce that they have arrived, or that someone died on the trip. He steers them clear of job brokers trying to rush immigrants into work contracts before they get their bearings. Usually these sly people offering train tickets and jobs are dealing in involuntary servitude.

Last, he gives them copies of the New Testament, written in Swedish and English. By reading the words of comfort they will learn the new language.

A high wooden fence encircles the building. We have gone from the shore through the center and so far have been isolated from the new environment. After leaving this protective wall, we are bombarded by the city and its people.

The buildings vary from brick with shiny fronts to shanties about to fall down. Well-dressed couples stroll down the avenue, ignoring the litter along the gutters. The aroma of fresh-baked bread mixes with the putrid stink of garbage.

People everywhere are trying to get us to part with our money.

"Buy your tickets here for trains to the West."

"Right this way folks, we got the best sausage in town!"

"Need a hotel for the night?"

Crowds crush together as the immigrants flood out of the center and citizens push in to hawk their wares. The street is teeming with people selling food, fares, newspapers, hope, and fantasy. I can't understand their language and the Pastor said to ignore even the salesmen speaking Swedish because they are countrymen that have turned unscrupulous. My thought is to protect our possessions and family so that neither is snatched from us.

Not all the rush is hostile. Reunions and farewells go on, oblivious to the passing scene. Good-bys are said to friends and families parting ways to seek work in different cities. Brothers reunite after years apart. Young women who have arrived to become brides embrace their intended husbands.

For some the journey has ended here in New York City, and for others, like us, the journey is only partway completed. The pastor herds his flock onto a ferry that crosses the Hudson River to the train terminal in New Jersey. We're already going into another state. How many more do we pass though to get to Illinois? Are all the states this close to one another? They look farther apart on the map in our handbook.

After the big trunk is stored at the depot, we make our way with children and luggage to a hotel near the train station. We'll rest a night, then start tomorrow morning for the next leg of our trip. Samuel asks, "Why aren't you excited? I thought you would be ecstatic that you're off the ship."

I try to explain that, yes, I'm glad that my mended shoes have touched American soil, but I'm tired and long for a bath, the children are cranky, and my swollen feet ache. Besides, it doesn't seem like we're "there" yet. I think of this as just another stop. I'm not unpacking our belongings from the big trunk, hanging up our clothes in our bedroom, fixing a meal on our hearth yet. We're not in our own home.

And I am disappointed by my first impression of America. Most Americans have been crude, indifferent to comfort (let alone sanitation), and think nothing of swindling innocent people. I don't feel safe. The children couldn't go out and play here. And I'm scared our money won't last. Then Samuel will leave us to find work and I'll have to fend for the family alone. Where are the trees, grass, and lush fields described in the pamphlets Samuel brought home from the meetings? No, so far I'm not impressed with America.

We've been uprooted for a life that will be forever different from what we left. Our ties with Sweden, our childhood, and our parents have been permanently severed. I'm among people whose actions and language I don't understand. And I'm homesick for Kulla and all we left behind.

A View of Green

"Three more days, Charlotta. Only three more days," promises Samuel.

He stuffs another piece of bread in his mouth while he scrapes the last spoonful of food out of the bowl.

Our first breakfast in America. Some lumpy concoction they call "oatmeal", a light-colored wheat bread, and coffee so weak I can see the bottom of the cup. I woke up this morning looking forward to a hot bowl of porridge, a thick slice of rye bread smothered with rich butter, and strong coffee with cream straight from the cow.

Food is not the same in America. They use different grains in their cooking and baking. We grew only rye on Kulla. Here we've been introduced to oats and wheat.

Next we'll have indigestion as we adjust.

I'm not ready to get back on a moving vehicle this morning, but we can't waste our money on hotels. We need to keep moving toward our destination. The next three days we will spend on an immigrant train headed for Chicago. The express train makes the trip from New York to Chicago in eighteen hours but is too costly for four people and our belongings. So we'll take the slow version with hundreds of other immigrants heading the same way.

It moves so slowly that I sometimes think I could walk faster than this old rattletrap is moving. We stop often on a side track and wait for an express train to whiz by—hours spent waiting that could have cut our travel time by a day. At least we can get

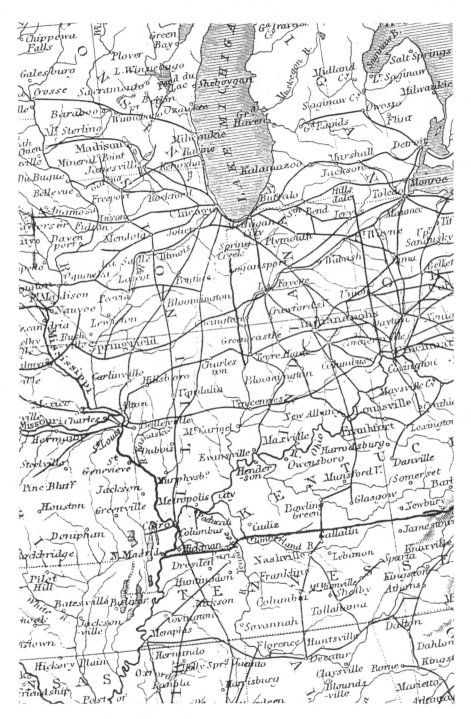

Eastern United States, circa 1800s

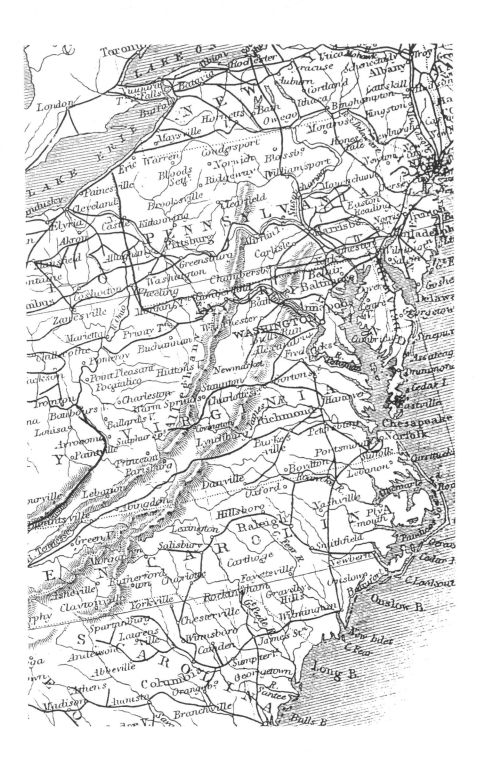

out, stretch, and get a bit of fresh air before being confined in the crowded train again.

The old cars have seen better days but have been put in service to transport the thousands of immigrants heading west. Bare-wood benches fill the interior of some, others are empty of seats and people have to sit on their trunks or the floor. All are hot and stuffy with too many people.

The end of May is much warmer here than at home. Sweat trickles down the inside front of my blouse even though I have removed my coat, vest, and extra petticoats. Emilia is breaking out in a rash from the heat. The stifling weather has made everyone uncomfortable and grumpy. I'm sure we'll adjust in time, but our Swedish woolen clothes have got to be exchanged for something cooler for this time of year here. It doesn't help that we're sitting on the side where the sun streams into the windows.

At least the scenery has improved. After going through slums and suburbs along the riverside of New Jersey, we eased into a panoramic view of green countryside. You could almost hear a sigh of relief through the car. Fortunately, all of America doesn't look like New York City. During our days of travel it has changed back and forth from country to city to little town.

As we chugged through the Pennsylvanian cities of Philadelphia, Harrisburg, and Pittsburgh, the factory smoke reminded me a little of Liverpool. Although there have been people in these cities for more than a century, people from different countries have migrated in to work in their industries. It wasn't just English we heard during stops in this state. These towns have pockets of people from various countries living next to one another.

The Germans we encountered were neat, orderly, and sober, helping us out if they could. I cringed when I heard an Irishman. It wasn't true of all of them, but some seemed to be unreliable and ill-tempered. The Yankees, as we found out the American northerners were called, bemused us with their bragging. We've had quite a lesson on humanity during our trip.

As we crossed America, we were impressed by its size and beauty. The country seemed endless. It varied from trees in the undisturbed mountain forests in Pennsylvania to lush green grass in the stonefree loam of the Indiana prairie. Rivers and lakes were swimming with fish, and innumerable birds flew overhead. It looked like the promised land to all of us.

The farmers on our train stared like children when we passed through farmland in Pennsylvania and Ohio. The homesteads featured two-story wooden houses, massive barns of timber and stone, and more outbuildings to hold livestock and machinery than we could imagine owning. Herds of workhorses grazed in pastures. Swedish farmers rarely own more than one or two horses and use oxen for their draft animals instead. Here it looked as if there was a pair of draft horses for every day of the week.

If someone was out working a field, it lead to a discussion of the farm machinery he was using, the type of crop being planted or mowed, and what kind of yield was expected.

One small depot we stopped at was right on the edge of a newly planted field. Half the train passengers charged to it like a magnet, kneeling to reverently touch the soil. A handful revealed dark loam that stuck together with the right amount of moisture. It wasn't a muddy clay ball or a sift of dust, like the two extremes we were used to. The people didn't want to disturb the planting but couldn't help carefully digging down into the first furrow on the edge of the field to see what seed was planted and how deep. They carefully recovered the healthy new roots that would easily reach the moisture needed to boost strong plants. There were no rocks here to stunt the growth or crack a plow.

This scene was repeated every time we made a rural stop. We marveled at the uniform germination of the fields. There were no bare or yellow spots in the plantings. The dark green color of the young corn looked like it came from pure fertilizer.

In one town there was an implement dealer across the street from the depot. Calloused hands caressed steel plows, legs folded to ease down into the seat of a two-row corn planter. Then we gulped at the prices. The hand-rake harvester cost more than two hundred dollars and the mower was a hundred and twenty-five. Some of the immigrants didn't have that much hidden in their money belts! We thought American farmers *must* be rich, just look at the farms we've passed and all the equipment lined up by the granaries. Farming seemed to pay so well that soon we could own one of everything, too. We couldn't wait to get to Illinois to see the land we hoped to call our own. Soon we, too, would be wealthy American farmers with a stable of horses and a yard full of machinery.

The two nights we spent sleeping in or outside, around the train depots. It was uncomfortable and noisy with snoring and children crying, but it was cheap. The money we saved could go toward purchasing one of those new steel plows for our farm.

We didn't eat in any restaurants on this leg of the journey but bought food from vendors who were set up by the depots. We could buy fresh milk, meat, bread, and some early garden vegetables. The more rural the depot, the better and fresher the food was.

According to our map, we cut across the middle of three states before angling up to Chicago. Towns I remember in Ohio were Mansfield and Lima, and Fort Wayne and Plymouth, Indiana. Most towns had a sign posted before we pulled up to the station or on the side of the depot building. The one I was wanting to see would say "Andover, Illinois."

Quite a number of our fellow travelers departed in Chicago, including the Pettersons. Some had relatives they were meeting, others thought this was the perfect town to find employment because there were supposed to be many Swedes already settled here. I felt it was just another big city with a mass of people. Yes, it was a comfort that many spoke our language, but I didn't want to live in a crowded tenement building on a noisy street when we knew there was open land available elsewhere.

I won't be surprised if Hedda goes back to Chicago if she can't find housework in Andover. There were some impressive homes there that would hire domestic help. But she wants to see where we settle first and try to find something near us.

Finally we switch trains, and we're on the last part of our journey. We watch the signs as they go by: Aurora, Mendota, Buda, and Galva. Farms dot the landscape between towns, but they seem to be far apart. Is there land available between the farmsteads, or are they all that big? The buildings don't look as big and impressive as in Pennsylvania.

Where is the open prairie where we get to homestead free land? Maybe it's on the other side of Andover.

Our anticipation builds as the conductor says we get off at the next stop. Children and parents are both excited that our journey is over.

"Put your coats and hats back on. We must look presentable as we step off the train. This is our new home, children. Yes, we're finally here. No more traveling. Yes, I promise we'll be in a real home soon."

But the depot sign says "Galesburg." We know it is a big Swedish community, but why are we being told to get off? We had planned to step off the train in Andover.

Portion of Henry County, Illinois, circa 1877

Look for the Steeple

"At least we have a roof over our heads and I have a job through the winter." Samuel is trying to convince himself that even though things didn't work out as we had hoped, we will not starve. A week of worry preceded our finding this place, though.

Our dreams had built up so big during our journey that we expected to walk off the train, pick our land practically from the train platform, pay cash for all we needed, and set up housekeeping by nightfall. Of course we didn't expect it to be that easy, but America was the place where all our dreams were to come true.

Reality set it quickly. Two carloads of bewildered people unloaded at Galesburg. Now what? Where do we and fifty other people find a place to live—starting with tonight's lodging? Can we find a hotel with a cheap rate, or are we allowed to sleep at the depot until we find a room?

Everyone is hungry. Traveling costs have whittled at the savings that was supposed to last much longer. How many more meals before we are out of money?

Immediate employment is needed to continue feeding the family, but look at all these men standing on the platform in the same dire situation. All the farmers on this train are going to be vying for a piece of farmland in this area. And how many trainloads of immigrants came before us this spring looking for the same thing? Panic overtakes me. Now that we are here, what do we do?

The depot agent is patient, considering he is asked these same questions daily. "Talk to Pastor Dahlsten at the First Lutheran Church. He'll help you find a place to stay tonight and a meal to fill your stomachs," he says as he points up the street. "Follow north on Prairie Street several blocks, then go right on Waters Street until you see the white wooden building. The church is good about giving you a hand."

"But, sir, we want to go to Andover."

"Well, that's twenty-five miles on north. Tomorrow morning you come back here and ride to Lynn Center, then you're on your own. Check with their livery to see if you can hire a wagon to get to Andover."

We were not at our final destination after all. We wander with the crowd to the church mentioned, looking for food and advice. We've now among fellow Swedes, but we're just the latest throng of immigrants that have arrived. Will they help us or resent us for moving in on their town and their charity?

"Go due west. It's only about three miles. Keep looking for a high church steeple in the distance. That's what the locals call the 'Cathedral on the Prairie.' It's the new Lutheran church being built in the middle of Andover. Call on Pastor Swenson when you get there. He'll show you over to the Immigrant House."

We're closer, but still not there.

It was a short train ride. It took longer to load our baggage in Galesburg and unload it at Lynn Center than to ride there. At the time I was thinking that I'll be glad when we don't have to travel with all our possessions anymore.

Besides us, there were two other families who got off at Lynn Center. After we hired a wagon it was brought to the depot to load our belongings. We split the cost, but with three families' luggage there wasn't room for passengers. So we walked beside the wagon, looking for our landmark.

In some ways, our walking seems fitting for the final leg of our journey. We're farmers, tuned to the rhythm of the land, and our stroll is the perfect way to get acquainted with this new area.

All our senses are close to the earth to witness nature. We saw the scenery through the window of the train car, but walking makes us part of that view.

The land rolls slightly; it's not perfectly flat like some of the land we crossed earlier. Edges of the native prairie are still visible between fields of green. There are some pockets of deciduous trees in the landscape, but nothing like Sweden with its pine and birch forests.

The air is sweet with warm earth and blooming weeds along the trail. We've breathed all kinds of city pollution in the last two weeks, and I welcome the fresh scent of the countryside. A bird call in the distance mixes in with the steps of the foot travelers and team. A grasshopper clinging to the top of a blade of tall grass chirps as it sways in the breeze.

We stop partway to rest. The children are tired of trying to keep up with their little legs, and the heat and humidity is difficult for all of us. There is a bit of breeze, but the sweat is trickling down my back.

A farmstead sits close to the road where we stop. It's not a big place like some we've seen. It doesn't look very old, but most of the buildings could use some repair and a coat of paint. It probably was one of the first homesteads built when the area was established twenty years ago. The only trees on the place are fruit varieties west of the house.

We don't see any activity around it, and we wonder if it is vacant. All the windows and doors in the small house appear shut. They should be open with today's heat. The porch faces the road, and there are tall weeds mixed with wilting daisies along its edge. You'd think the farmwife would pull the weeds to enjoy the flowers.

The barn is modest by most standards. The pen next to the barn is empty. There are no grunts of pigs echoing from behind the pig shed or chickens scratching around the buildings. The field beyond the barn is planted with corn, so the ground is not idle. There is a stretch of native prairie behind the barn that is ready to be mowed for hay.

Samuel goes up to the house to see if we can draw water from the well we see in the farmyard, but no one answers his knock. Even though the top of the well is covered, the bucket is still hanging inside. So he draws water for us to drink.

We sit on the porch during our break. Samuel had lifted the food basket from the wagon to get cups, so I gave the children some food. Revived somewhat, the group of youngsters chase one another around the yard until it is time to leave. When we're done, I pour the last of the water on the daisy clump by the steps.

If I lived here, I'd draw water from this well every morning to water these flowers.

So this is Andover.

Swedes from Kalmar *Län* settled here during the early years of Swedish migration to America. Kristbala, about twenty-five miles southeast of Pelarne, lost nearly half of its four thousand citizens when they moved to the Andover area in the last decade. Now we get to see what they wrote home about in their letters. I expected a much larger town, but its relatively small size is a comfort after the big cities we've been in. I'll feel much safer here than in places like New York or Chicago.

People and vehicles are coming and going on their errands around town. Dogs chase playing children. Although bare of trees along the dirt streets, the town appears clean. It looks like a nice place to live.

The church and pastor were easy to find. He walked with us the three blocks to the immigrant shelter. Along the way he pointed out businesses, residents, and gave us a history of the town. It started with a few Englishmen in 1835. They have a mill down south of town on the Edwards River. Swedes came to the area in the 1840s and started a commune south of here named Bishop Hill. Starting with around one thousand immigrants in the beginning, it amassed over twelve thousand acres by the early 1860s. Huge brick buildings were built to house people and businesses. The commune was dissolved and the land was divided among the members in 1861. Dissenters, and new immigrants who followed later, raised the Swedish population of neighboring towns.

A group led by a Pastor Esbjörn came to Andover in 1850, but they had a hard time building their first church because of cholera epidemics. They started the little white chapel in 1851, with funds the pastor collected from people in the East. Jenny Lind, the Swedish singer, gave him fifteen hundred dollars for the fund.

Progress wasn't made during the next two years. The church basement was used for a hospital and the grounds sheltered hundreds of immigrants that kept arriving.

At the height of the cholera epidemic wagons went around the colony daily to pick up the dead, which were buried in mass trenches north of the church. When the church was finished in 1854, it was without a steeple because the lumber purchased for the steeple had been used for coffins instead.

Within a decade the expanding congregation didn't fit the chapel any more, so construction on the new church nearby started last year. Members made over fifty thousand bricks for it. It seats one thousand people. The inside is not finished, but there is a temporary altar, pulpit, and benches. The building rivals the big-city churches we saw on our trip. I think they made up for the lost steeple, because the one on the new church is one hundred and thirty-six feet tall.

Besides the Lutheran church, there is also a Methodist and a Presbyterian church. The tidy appearances of the hotel and downtown businesses prove the town is flourishing. The two-story school is empty this time of year but nevertheless shows there must be a budding population of children in town. We already passed a country school on the way from Lynn Center, so we know education will be available for our children wherever we settle.

It was strange to see a young town. Andover was started less than forty years ago. I don't think I had ever been in a building that new in Sweden, let alone a town.

We pestered the Pastor with questions about available land in the area. Samuel's shoulders sagged when he heard there is no homesteading land in this area, and probably not in the state. All the prairie sod was broken up over a decade ago. Farms are prospering now that they are well established. If a place does go up for sale, the going price is high. There were groups talking about banding together and moving farther west next spring. If we couldn't find land here, we could move on.

The best the Pastor could recommend was that Samuel ask around to find employment in a business in town, or for a job as a farmhand. Word circulated when something came up, but with so many people looking for jobs, the competition was fierce and the pay low.

Pastor Swenson brought us to a residence that is being used as an immigrant haven. We can stay here while Samuel looks for work and a place to live. I wonder how long we'll be allowed to stay, because I'm worried it might take a while to get settled.

This morning we walked the boardwalk on the main street and peered in store windows to get familiar with what business are in town. We'll be living here, so we need to learn about what is here.

We found the post office. I suggested we send a letter back to Sweden to let family know we arrived safely, but Samuel said he wants to wait until he has good news. He wants to tell his *fader* about his new Illinois farm. I just let it pass for now. We both know that owning a farm here is beyond our means, but we don't want to admit it to ourselves or to family just yet.

Samuel will soon find out for himself if land is available. The land agent was in his office, so Samuel made for the door. I would like to have been in on the conversation but sense this is something Samuel wants to do without an audience. He wants to face the disappointing news by himself. Hedda and I steer the children down the street to the next shop so the men can talk in private.

The large plate glass windows of the mercantile shine, beckoning us to come and see what's inside. The door stands open, with mixed aromas from food to leather drifting out. After living in Sweden's lean years, it is comforting to see shelves stocked full, bulk produce in barrels, and cured meat hanging from the ceiling. The store has everything from tools to household goods to furnish the home and farm.

The shelves are stocked with cans and boxes with labels in English. We can guess the contents of some by the picture on the labels, but of others we have no clue. How will we know if a medicine will cure or poison us if we can't read the words? But this store has rye flour and salted herring at the request of homesick Swedes. It is nice to be able to speak Swedish with the clerk.

Hedda ran her hand against the bolts of bright printed calico on a shelf. I know she longs for a new dress of cooler material. Don't women weave their own fabric here?

"Yes, we're new in town," I say to the clerk, and, "No, I don't know where we are going to live yet." He seems to have more confidence than I do that our situation will reverse soon.

Little hands quickly grab the stick candy the clerk hands them. I'm horrified when they stick it in their mouths, because now I must pay for it. I have few coins on me and no idea how much the candy costs. The grinning man assures me it is a free treat for the children, and I smile a "thank you" in relief. Every coin in our possession has been counted more than once, and it is painful to part with each one.

After Samuel spent a week looking for a job in this town and the neighboring areas, his luck turned around. A Mr. Peterson came to the immigrant house looking for Samuel. He had a vacant farm and he needed an experienced person to take over the place for this next growing season.

"I can't promise you it would be a permanent place, because I might put it on the market. But the family that rented the farm left for the West recently, and with all the field work needing to get done, I need someone to move in right away. I haven't had the time to look for someone to take care of the place until now. I asked Pastor Swenson to be on the lookout for a family he thought might be suitable, and he mentioned you.

"Actually, if you came to Andover by way of Lynn Center, you went by the farm. It's on the north side about a mile back, a small house that sits close to the road."

That's the farm where we stopped for water.

Samuel hesitates, not knowing whether we should take this offer or wait for something better. It would be only a temporary place, but what if we can't find anything else?

I nod my head to Samuel's puzzled stare. I think this will work for our first home in America. Besides, I've already sat on the porch and watered the flowers.

Tending Time and Crops

We finally have a roof over our heads and a way to provide food and income. Our possessions were hauled to the farm and I was back on the porch, ready to make this house our home.

The white wood-frame house consisted of a rectangle-shaped kitchen, which you stepped into from the porch, then a living room and a bedroom on the east. A flight of stairs just off the bedroom ran upstairs to two small dormer bedrooms. It was sparsely furnished with table, chairs, beds, the basic necessities to make do.

The first thing Hedda and I did was to scrub the house from top to bottom. Although it had not been vacant for very long, it was musty from being closed up. It wasn't in a filthy state, but I felt everything needed to be cleaned because someone else's scent and dirt was in it. Curtains were taken down and washed. The woodstove, which I had to get used to cooking with, was cleaned of its old ashes and polished. I even scrubbed the porch to remove the road dust.

Unpacking did not take long because we brought so little with us. The rug found a place in the kitchen by the front door, not by a hearth. Dishes, cooking utensils, and the staples we bought in Andover were stored on the open cupboard shelves. The bedding was washed, dried in the sunshine, and heaven to sleep in after our varied accommodations over the past weeks. The children's clothing had stains that needed attention. Our good clothes and coats were brushed and stored in the trunk we unloaded.

There were no treasures to display in the living room. Looking at bare shelves made me yearn for the things I left behind. "Wouldn't the clock have looked nice there? That picture still hanging in the living room in Sweden could have hung on that wall." I knew it would take time to find things for the house, but at times I was impatient to have a house that looked like a home.

Samuel, with Oscar tagging along, spend his first days cleaning up the farmyard. Overgrown weeds around the perimeter of the house and outbuildings had to be chopped down. Manure was pitched out of the barn. Samuel cleaned the tool shed just as fervently as I cleaned the house. Tools were unpacked and hung on one wall.

The squawking of chickens caught our attention at dawn the second morning. The man who owned the farm pulled up to the barn with a coop of chickens in the back of his wagon and had a cow and a saddled horse tied behind. He had brought this livestock for us.

The laying hens and the ruffled rooster scattered when freed from their cage. Within minutes their squawks of panic had turned to clucks of content as they scratched the ground for food.

Oh, to have a milk cow again! It wasn't just the need for milk and cream that I was happy to have, but I had missed the routine of milking. The time I spent in those early morning hours was mine alone to dream and think in.

The pair of Percheron draft horses was unhitched from the wagon and turned into the small pasture off the barn. The harnesses were hung in the barn and the wagon was parked beside it. Samuel couldn't have been more excited, although he tried not to show it. Never had he had such fine animals to work with. Oxen had been the main work animal on our Swedish farm, and I knew the horses would spoil him as much as he would them.

Although Samuel was hoping the gelding bay would stay, the farmer had brought it to ride back home.

The two men spent the rest of the morning discussing equipment that was in place on the farm. They walked the fields, looking at the progression of the crops, talking about what needed to be done next—this patch of broom corn will be the first to cultivate, the hay should be cut next week if it doesn't look like rain.

While watching them from the living room window, I wondered what Samuel must have been thinking. This is all so new to him—the crops, the machinery, working with horses. I could tell from the house that he looked a little apprehensive. Asking questions and doing his best is all he can do. I could also tell that Samuel wished that this farm was his own place, with its growing crops and livestock. The farmer was very kind compared to some Swedish landowners we've known, but I'm sure Samuel was thinking that, even though people are very generous here, he was still a farmhand working for someone else.

We slipped into the routine of summer. The corn seemed to grow overnight in the humid hot air that takes over the state this time of year. Samuel toiled to keep the weeds clear of the rows. Not only did he need to earn his pay, but he also needed to learn about the crops that are grown in America.

I tended the garden we started by the well. Fresh vegetables spoiled us after last summer's barren harvest. We couldn't afford the jars Americans use to keep fruit, so I dried the peaches, plums, and apples we harvested from the orchard trees. Everything we stored will feed our family this winter.

I worked on these projects alone because Hedda found a housekeeping position in town. She had Sundays free, so she came out to the farm after church service to eat dinner with us and play with the children. The afternoons we spent sitting out on the porch to escape the heat of the house. I stayed isolated on the farm that summer with the children and rarely was in town. Hedda, on the other hand, was part of the social life of Andover and enjoyed the easy work of housekeeping. She was picking up English words that she taught to us. The children seemed to mimic Hedda and learn faster than I did. We tried to learn the language because we didn't know where we would be moving next. Very few American towns have so many Swedes as Andover.

We were satisfied with life on our rented farm until mid-August. Through the church we heard that there was a meeting the first of that month in Galesburg to organize a committee to look for land farther west to start a new Swedish community.

This might be our opportunity to start our own farm. And suddenly visions of moving again filled our thoughts as we tended the rented land and milked the borrowed cow. Passing time and the meetings about moving west helped my restlessness grow. I didn't want to become attached to the house and community knowing we would have to leave it. Samuel kept looking but couldn't find a farm we could afford to buy. Maybe if we spent several years renting a place we could eventually save enough money to buy a small acreage, but land prices are going to continue to increase as the farms in this area mature.

Samuel went to another meeting a week later where there must have been three to four hundred men. You can tell this area is too crowded when that many families are looking for land. There were hundreds of displaced immigrants in western Illinois trying to find work and homes. Something had to be done to help the immigrants, so action was being taken. They formed a committee of five men that will scout out possible land in Missouri, Kansas, and Nebraska.

The goal of the Galesburg group was to find enough land for an entire group of people to move at one time. There have been advertisements in the newspaper about river-valley land for sale in the state of Kansas. Railroads were given land on alternating sections of the planned route to lay the track. Once the route has been chosen, the excess land is being offered for sale for reasonable prices.

The committee came back with good news. They had looked over land in Missouri first but didn't find anything to their liking. Then they went on to the Smoky Hill River Valley in central Kansas. Pastor Dahlsten had a letter from a fellow Swedish pastor, Olof Olsson, who had contracted land in that area for a group coming from Chicago. Our committee liked the land and decided to settle next to the Chicago group to form a larger Swedish community. They contracted to buy twenty-two sections of land, or fourteen thousand eighty American acres. The price will range from a dollar fifty an acre for upland sections to five dollars for bottom land.

To make the land selection as fair as possible, a lottery was held to find out what land a family would settle on. Each section was drawn as a unit. Family and friends who wished to live on adjoining farms drew one unit. Each section will hold four to eight families, depending on whether they want eighty or a hundred and sixty acres. One person from each unit drew a slip of paper from a jar that listed their section's legal coordinates. The contract for the land would require a fifth of the total for a down payment and four other equal payments at ten percent interest. Only the interest is due the first year.

So many families wanted to move that a committee member had to go back to Kansas to contract for another thirty-eight thousand acres. The Sandberg, Brodine, and Gustafson families we met at church were just a few we knew who were moving. Pastor Dahlsten from Galesburg is going to set up a church for the new community.

We decided to move with the group. We still want land of our own, and this was the perfect opportunity. We will be with people from our native country that speak our language and uphold the customs we are used to. Most of the families are from the Kalmar and Dalarna areas of Sweden.

Samuel didn't participate in the lottery because we want to homestead free land near the contracted tract. The money we save on the land could go to building materials, seed, and equipment. Hedda decided to stick with the family and come along.

The first group left for the Kansas prairie in October. Others followed in small groups until a whole trainload moved in February. We planned to leave early this spring, but then a letter from Sweden delayed our departure. Mathilda kept the vow she made a year ago. She would be traveling to Illinois in May.

Moving this time will not be so hard. Yes, there are more things to pack, but we know what to expect. The two-day train ride will be easy compared to our three-week journey a year ago. I've started piling up things that can be packed ahead. Mathilda should be arriving any day, so we plan to leave soon after she comes.

Clothes for the five of us will be folded and packed back in the trunk that made the trip from Sweden. Bedding will be stuffed in sacks. Household goods accumulated over the past year will fit into two crude crates Samuel made from cheap lumber. I wish I could take this stove with me. I have used up the staples so we don't have to pay for their weight. We will buy new food supplies in the town near our new land. What dried fruit is left I'll take along because we won't have an established orchard. We have definitely accumulated material goods this past year.

The *brudkista* will transport the valuables. I decided to pack it today in order to get it done. Our wedding quilt is wrapped around the picture frame Samuel made for me to hang in the living room. In the frame I stretched an embroidered sampler of the Swedish table prayer I had stitched as a child. The wooden spoon and knife set that Samuel carved for my engagement gift are there, along with the few china plates and cups I've managed to trade for eggs at the general store. And a bundle of letters, the link to family at home. I mentally correct myself as I tuck the letters in the chest. America is our home now. Time has improved my *hemlängtan*—until another letter arrives. Then I pine for my old home again.

They have been read, reread, and will be kept and cherished. Just touching the same paper that they held brings a flood of memories each time I hold it. I can see Fader sitting at the table discussing what to write before he even puts the pen in the ink. Moder is sitting in the chair by the fireplace telling him what to write while knitting socks. They will reread the last letter we sent to make sure they have answered all our questions, then they discuss ones to ask us. I imagine Johannes and Stina are sometimes there to add their input. Then the task of laboring over the the actual writing comes. Between the times that they read the letters, I imagine the pages are stored in a special memento box on top of the mantel.

It was months before we got the first letter. First they had to receive the letter Samuel sent to them saying that we had settled in Andover, Illinois. Samuel's letter started formally, just stating the fact that we all arrived safe and hearty. No, we haven't bought land but have rented a farm near Andover for a year. But I knew the parents would want to know how the trip was, how long it took, did we have any trouble? We went into details of the area, of the farm we were renting, and made comparisons of America and Sweden.

Then we had our own questions. Has it rained? How are the crops doing? Were they still healthy? Any neighborhood gossip of friends and family we left behind?

I couldn't help but reach back in the chest and pull out the first letter we received from them.

Dear Family,

We received your letter postmarked June 1 from Andover, Illinois, U.S.A. We think of you being so far away, but here a letter comes, retracing your route. I think Moder carried the letter round in her pocket for a week, touching it often, just because you had handled the paper before her. She doesn't say much, but I know she mourns the lost of her daughters and grandchildren, just like I do.

We're glad to hear you found a place to live. It sounds like such a fine place. Describe it in more detail so we can picture the farm. How close to town is it?

How has the weather been this summer? It continues to be hot and dry here. The grain shriveled before it got knee high. I'm afraid we are in for another famine year.

What kinds of crops will you be harvesting this fall? You wrote about broom corn and sorghum. What are they used for? How many acres will you harvest? Will you have help, or does the American machinery you described take the place of extra hands? I'd love to drive the team of dependable horses you are working with. You must get your work done twice as fast and cover twice the field. With all those acres to take care of, be glad you're not plodding behind our slow old oxen.

I can't believe you haven't found a rock on the place! I moved several before forenoon coffee and think about your absence of stone every time I leaned over!

Moder asks how are the children, and Hedda. We haven't gotten a letter from her describing her new job yet. And how are you feeling, Lotta? We hope the trip wasn't too strenuous for the unborn child.

We miss you, but I must say you made the right decision to leave because you wouldn't have made any income from the farm again this year.

Please write as soon as you can. Moder needs to hear from you again.

Much love and prayers,

Your parents

Our letters to our parents described in more detail the farm and its production because that was what interested them the most. Even though we were on different land in different countries, farming was the tie that bound us. Each letter asked more questions on weather and growing conditions. When do you harvest oats? How much hay do you get per acre? What is the average amount of rainfall in July? Some things we didn't know ourselves until we experienced them, but we tried to answer each question and more. Our description of thunderstorms that lit up the sky with brilliant jolts of lightning and blasted the farm with a burst of hailstones caused them to write back in alarm. They were not only worried about us but about the crops they had tended through our letters.

When Johannes wrote the letter, different questions were asked, mainly because of his ties to the church. Are you going to church there? Did you hand over your transfer papers and join yet? Have you made arrangements for the new child to be baptized as soon as it is born?

We assured them we were a part of the Andover Lutheran Church congregation, but we have not joined because of our temporary situation. The churches here are the social as well as the spiritual centers of the community. We have met people that have become like family, because most are transplanted from Sweden.

When the leaves of the sugar maple and ash turned colors this fall, I pressed and sent a leaf of each in our letters home. The autumn weather was warm during the days, but had a crisp scent to it that was hard to describe. Nights cooled down just as soon as the early sunset disappeared over the horizon.

The harvest pace intensified as damp cold weather threatened the community. Farmers helped one another cut and bale the broom corn on their neighboring acreages. Wagonloads were carted to processing plants, where the seed was stripped from the tops and the brooms sorted.

Samuel mastered working with draft horses and the machinery used in the harvest. It was still hard work but so much faster compared to the old Swedish ways.

Frost hit the garden one morning in early October, covering the vines with sparkling crystals. We harvested plump orange pumpkins and bushels of turnips from the garden and stored them in the root cellar. I wrote an inventory list of all the food we had harvested for our winter supply, wishing I could send half my stored produce to my family in Sweden.

Just as in Sweden we cut wood for the winter, repaired buildings so they would protect those inside from the cold to come, and gave thanks for the harvest. And we also wrote the news that we would be moving to Kansas in the spring to homestead land.

In our Christmas letter we described the new granddaughter, Josefina Mathilda, born to us on December 12. Our new friends, August and Elizabeth Sandberg, were her sponsors on her baptism six days later. Josefina wore the christening gown Moder snuck in the trunk right before we left.

We assured the family that all three children were adjusting to their new home, were healthy and growing, and would enjoy Christmas, even though they would miss their grandparents.

Christmas preparations in our area was the same as in Sweden. *Lutfisk* and *sill* were available at the general store. *Julotta* was celebrated at the church. I did tell them that Oscar and Emilia had been worried that the *jultomte* couldn't find them this Christmas because they had moved. But a storekeeper in Andover assured them that the Swedish Christmas elf has always found his way to this Swedish community.

The early snows with blowing wind seemed colder than Sweden in December, and I couldn't help mentioning that in the letter. I tried not to be melancholy, but I'm sure they guessed that we were homesick for the Christmas season in Pelarne. Even though we were among countrymen, Christmas would be sad without family sharing a meal, presenting gifts, giving one another an embrace of good wishes.

I enclosed seeds in an early spring letter so our mothers could start patches of daisies by their front steps, along with a few kernels of broom corn for our fathers to plant. We knew they would enjoy watching something grow that we had tended in America. This would be our last letter from Illinois. The next would be mailed from Kansas.

I'm look up from my reading to glance out the living room window. Two girls carrying suitcases are walking down the road toward Andover. Being close to the road, we have gotten used to the traffic and hardly pay attention to travelers. Now, opposite our house, the two plop down beside the road, apparently to rest before continuing to their destination. They look hot, so I decide to be hospitable and take water out to them. When the porch door slammed behind me, the two looked my direction.

One of the girls sitting in the ditch is my sister Mathilda.

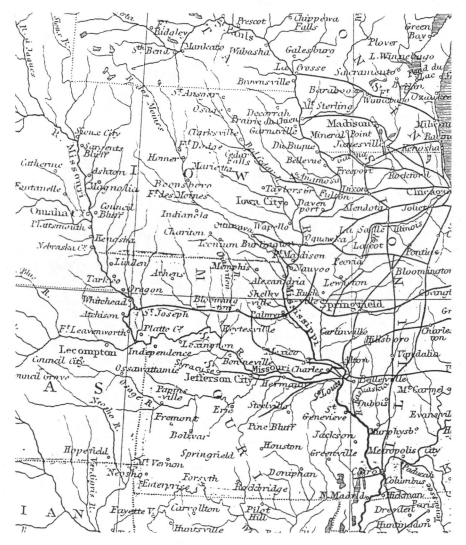

Route from Illinois to Kansas, circa 1800s

Open Prairie

Mathilda is not traveling with us to Kansas. When our train pulled away from the Lynn Center station yesterday morning, she was sitting in the depot waiting for the next train east. When she and her friend traveled through Chicago they found work and were here just for a visit. We only had three days to catch up on a year's worth of visiting. Mathilda almost went hoarse telling Hedda and me all the news from home. We had so many questions. How are our parents? Are they going to get any harvest this year? Where is Johan working now? Sofia turns thirteen this fall. Is she starting to fill out? Who else from our parish left for America?

I hated to leave Mathilda behind in Illinois, but it will be exciting for her to experience life in a big city. Maybe after our settlement is established she'll follow us to Kansas. Right now she wants to explore America on her own.

Now we're seeing a new part of America. After switching trains at Galesburg, we headed southwest toward the state line. It is around four hundred and fifty miles to our destination.

The first hundred miles' scenery was similar to Andover's. Rows of young corn surrounded established farms. The depot signs are different each time, but all the towns have main-street businesses and steepled churches.

Many of the people at the Quincy, Illinois, depot were travelers coming or going from the river docks. Instead of the European immigrants we traveled with on our last train ride, we rubbed elbows with riverboat captions, freed slaves, and many others heading west for land.

The train crossed the Mississippi River on a long trestle bridge after leaving Quincy. I think it was the largest river we crossed on this trip. It was so wide that there were cargo boats and ships traveling the muddy water like it was a busy highway. Not too many years ago the train did not travel past the river and everyone had to take boats across the river to West Quincy, Missouri, to continue by stagecoach or wagon. Civilization is moving west as fast as transportation can take it.

The Missouri farms grew younger the farther we traveled. Some were just being rebuilt. Because of the Civil War conflicts along the Missouri and Kansas borders, farms in these areas were raided, set fire, and abandoned. Four years later the original farmers came back to start over, or new homesteaders moved in. The new barn styles are different from the ones built when the area was first plowed decades ago. Homes vary from new wood-frames to crude shacks. There is more grassland and cattle. The scenery changed from a flat landscape to rolling hills with sections of trees. Missouri has a wild look to it, like it fought back at being tamed.

It was twilight when we pulled into Carrollton, Missouri, for our night's stay. We had left mild weather and clean neat farms in Illinois and arrived in a windy heat that was as wild as the Missouri countryside. It made me wonder what we will find when we cross the Kansas line. I got my answer after chugging across the Missouri River bridge in Kansas City. More of the same, both in the weather and the lay of the land.

Pockets of homesteads surround the young towns in the eastern third of the state. Most of the land is homesteaded, but not all the prairie land has been plowed yet. Stands of oats and spring wheat are as common as corn.

We traveled through Topeka, Lawrence, and Manhattan, all established by Americans from the East when the territory opened in the middle 1850s. The train more or less followed the Kansas River, whose banks these towns have been built on. Tree groves of walnut and oak cluster along its edge, providing lumber and fuel for the area.

Then the land rolls into big hills of grass. Someone said the area was called the Flint Hills for the white limestone rock we saw in places. The land must not be suited for farming, because it was still open prairie when we saw it.

I'm ready to get off this hot stuffy train. We are getting close to our destination and I'm getting as restless as the children to get out of this car. Josefina has slept in my arms most of the day, but Emilia didn't take a nap and is getting overly tired. Oscar and Hedda are playing a guessing game to pass the time. Samuel is visiting with the gentleman sitting across the aisle.

This fellow traveler is a cattle trader from Illinois. His destination is Abilene, where his family runs a cattle operation. Wanting to know about our next stop, Samuel asks the man about the town and how it got started.

Abilene began in 1861 on the military road between Fort Riley and the western frontier. Within the last two years it has become a major shipping terminal for the beef industry. Because of the Texas fever these cattle carry, they are driven by foot up a quarantine zone from Texas, then shipped by rail to the eastern states. The man said that over fifty thousand head passed through Abilene last year. To accommodate the cattle and the men who work with them, there is a two hundred and fifty-acre stockyard adjacent to the rail line with its own barn, livery stable, offices, bank, and hotel.

Business establishments in Abilene evolve around this industry. Grocery houses do a booming business because food is sold in bulk and taken out to the incoming outfitters. Herders camp for days on the outlying prairies, waiting their turn to bring their cattle to the rail.

A lot of clothing is sold after the cowboys finish their two-month drive. After getting paid, the first place the cowboys visit is the barber shop, then the clothing store. Saloons, existing just for the purpose of selling hard liquor and entertainment, are the other places these herders spend their money.

After the quiet rolling countryside we have a lot to view during our short stop in Abilene. From one side of the car we can see the stockyards, and from the other side the hotel that is across the street from the depot.

The dust and smell rising from the animals penetrate the train car as we pull into town. There are more cattle here than we would ever expect to see in a dozen lifetimes. And the trader said there aren't many cattle here yet because it is only the first of the season. They have such long horns! They have to average six feet in length. The cows' horn tips curve up, but the bulls' grow almost horizontal. How do they get them in the railcars? Their hides are every color imaginable, but the spotted dull red seems to be the most common.

There aren't quite as many cowboys as cattle, but there are dozens sitting along the long hotel verandah. We guess the three-story Drover's Cottage is the hotel where they stay while in town.

The cowboys wear different clothes than Samuel does. The shirts and coats are similar, but cowboys wear denim or army pants instead of homespun, with revolvers hanging from a waist gunbelt. We were warned not to get out here because a sudden drunken brawl usually means a flash of violence. The cattle trader said the disorder was growing to a point where something needed to be done about it soon.

What a difference between Andover and Abilene. Yesterday we left a quiet Swedish community with three churches, and now we're in a rowdy cattle town with half a dozen saloons.

What will Salina be like?

Towering clouds are building above the prairie floor. They look like they could fall over on our train and smother us with their strength. The vast emptiness of the enormous prairie is frightening after living in the settled landscapes of Sweden—and Illinois, for that matter.

We're going to be living here—out in the middle of nowhere, subject to the elements, whether it be the burning summer sun, violent hailstorms, tornadoes, or prairie fires—without a shelter. Oh, I wish I could magically move everything from the rented farm to here, house and chicken coop included. That Illinois homestead spoiled us. Now we'll be moving out on the prairie with almost nothing—except our desire to build a new home. We know the land has potential, it's just up to us to develop it into a profitable farm.

The train engine slows down for our last stop. The depot sign says "Salina". I have been looking for that sign for two days—no, for one year. We have traveled over five thousand miles to find free land, and it is supposed to be near here.

Salina was just an outpost along the military road until after the Civil War. When the railroad tracks were laid to Salina in 1867 the town started to grow. The place still has a dirty windblown look to it, but new houses and businesses will make a difference.

While making arrangements to move out to our new land, we're staying at the Pacific Hotel. Hedda is looking for employment in town. Although I could use Hedda's help, she needs to earn money for herself. She'll come out to our new farm when we get settled.

Our first business this morning is to find John Johnson, the land agent for the area. Because he was involved in the Galesburg Land Company purchase, he will know what land has been contracted.

He spreads out the map of the county to point out sites that are available. What's our choice? Is there still good homestead land available, or are we too late? What does the land look like? Where is the nearest water supply? Are there creeks and trees in that area? Which section is best, which part of the section? Do we want to be on a corner or in the middle? Any idea where the church and school will be located, town plats laid out? We hope that a town closer than Salina will be built near our community, and we don't want to be too far away from it. How far is the Galesburg land from here?

Do you know where the Sandbergs or Brodines settled? We knew them in Illinois.

I feel like I'm asking too many questions, but we can't just shut our eyes and point to a spot and casually say "We'll take it." We plan to live on this land for the rest of our lives.

Maybe we should buy land. Are there any locations still available near the land set aside for the church? If we bought eighty acres at the cheapest price it would cost one hundred and twenty dollars. How much money would that leave in our savings?

Not enough to afford it.

We stand in the general store trying to visualize what we need to buy. I could pick one of each item off the shelves. But so far I don't have the money, or the house to put the goods in.

What are we going to do for shelter until we get our house up, or should I say dug, for we're told there are no trees in the area and most settlers prepare a dugout for their first homes. How do we protect our belongings we haul out there when it storms? What does a tent cost?

Staples for the first meals—flour, salt, what else? I won't have any eggs because we don't have any chickens. Gun ammunition to supply the meat. Should we buy some salted pork?

"No, Emilia, we can't buy candy this time. Oscar, please hold Josefina so I can concentrate on my list."

I won't have a stove, so I will have to cook over a campfire. What do we use for firewood if there are no trees around? What about matches?

A shovel to turn the first sod. Did you pack your ax? I don't remember it being in the crate.

How much corn seed should we buy? How many acres can we manage to plant before it's too late in the season? Can we borrow someone's plow, or do you plan to plant directly into the sod this first year? Shall we plant some broom corn too? Does Salina have a processing plant where we can sell it?

Can we get a milk cow?

How are we going to get all this and our baggage out to our land? The price of wagons and teams are higher here than I thought.

My head is starting to pound. It is overwhelming—all the money we brought with us has almost disappeared in an hour of shopping.

Did we make the right decision to leave Illinois? Well, if I wonder that, what about immigrating from Sweden? I still miss our parents and feel guilty leaving them behind. But I must remember the reason we left both places.

When we walked back to the hotel, I could see down a short street to the edge of town. The street fades into the prairie. Any trace of the town is gone there. I stop and stare. My farmer's blood stirs at the sight of this unplowed land. It finally comes to me that we will be standing on our own piece of prairie tomorrow.

Central Kansas, 1876 (note wrong placement of river)

Our Own Land

We were walking south this morning as the sun started to rise. The sun's pink in the east horizon faded to blue as we left Salina. A trace of moon was still visible in the sky. No more than a slight breeze stirred the air. My skirt absorbed the dew from the knee-high grass until I could wring water out of it like a newly washed garment. It felt like it was going to be a cool morning, but it quickly changed as the sun continued to rise.

Then we turned southwest, following a faint trail of bent grass. As the first hour of walking went into the second, a slight breeze stirred in our path. We spend time listening to the rhythm of our steps, the rumble of the wagons, the chatter of young children. We hear murmur of couples talking, dreaming out loud of the new land we will see in a few hours.

What will our new land look like? Will we be lucky enough to have trees? Tall lush grass would point to fertile soil below. What if we are unlucky in our choice? Can we trade the acreage for a different one? What if it is covered with rocks? How do we know we didn't pick something that is untillable?

How long will it take to build our dugout? We'll be living on the open prairie under the elements until it is completed. We will be sharing a plow with other farmers because most of us can't afford everything at once. How long will it take to turn sod so we can plant our first crop?

According to the map, we don't have any water running on our place. How deep will we have to dig the well in order to find the water?

Will we be able to live off the land when our store-bought supplies run out?

As we stop for a rest, I gaze to the southwest for the landmark that will announce our new home. On our first break the Smoky Buttes were not yet visible, but the second stop's location gave us a view of hazy blue hills in the distance. Two fellow Swedes that came to Salina to help our arrival talk in terms of size of acres and what they have done to their new patches, but it hasn't satisfied my curiosity about the feel and scent of the soil. I'm getting very anxious to end this twelve-mile walk.

The morning's clouds dissipate in an eternal blue sky. Sweat runs down under my sunbonnet as we trudge over the maze of grass. The morning sun is not in my eyes, but it heats up my dark clothing. The breeze that softly moves over the grass is not strong enough to dry my back. Most of the time my eyes are looking forward, or down to watch my path. Occasionally I glance to the west, looking at the buttes.

Then the shadowed hills of gray rise from the prairie floor. Although the heat has risen, so has our pace. Our new lives are waiting for us at the base of what we can see in the distance.

Then the shaded hills turn a bright green. The group stops again to stare at the change in scenery. The younger children are oblivious to us. They don't know that they are playing in the shadow of their new home, which they will inherit when their generation grows up.

Will Oscar remember his first look at the Buttes when this land becomes his?

Families break away from our group as they find their land. Three families stop on their section, and we move to the next section west.

"The land agent says this is ours? How can we tell?"

Our belongings are in another farmer's wagon. They are unloaded and piled on a bed of grass. We're standing on a level rise just east of a gap in the buttes. There is a gradual slope to the south. It blends in with the rest of the blowing grass. There are no roads, trails, or signs marking a visible boundary around what has become our eighty acres of land.

Our land. It slips off my tongue so easily. Our land, what we own in America.

The wind has picked up to become a constant siege. It whips my skirts between my legs, making it hard to walk. Emilia holds her arms out for balance. Her fingertips touch the grass that comes up to her waist. It is only the first of June. Another month and the grass will swallow her entirely.

"Well, what do you think Charlotta? Have we made a good choice?"

How do I feel about this land? As yet it is foreign to me, though similar to all the miles of prairie we have crossed over the last four hundred and fifty miles. What makes this land special?

I close my eyes and listen with my senses. Samuel and the children are silent, looking to me for the answer. At first I hear nothing but silence, but then the earth opens up. The wind whistles through the grass, a bird calls a short melody, even though there is not a tree in sight. The drone of insects rises as they go about their business. The damp soil gives off a rich earthy smell of moisture and life. The scents of pollinating grasses and wildflowers drift in and out of the air current as the wind blows them to me. I push back my sunbonnet to feel the wind blow wisps of hair around my temples while it dries the perspiration on my face.

I realize it has been a long time since I felt relaxed and at peace in my soul. We are finally at the end of our journey. I open my eyes to study the land in detail. It slowly comes to me that this is our grass, our soil, and our piece of earth, to take care of as long as we are able.

"Look at our new land, children."

I try to pull up a tuft of native grass but its roots are too deep in the soil. Beetles scurry for shelter after I disturb their hiding place. The pungent scent of yarrow arises when Oscar breaks off white flower heads from the soft mass of fronds. Emilia sneezes after shaking a stem of yellow clover that is as tall as she is. Golden honeybees effortlessly lift from one flower blossom to another to gather the rich nectar. Tiny plants two inches high are blooming just as well as the other wildflowers mixed within the grass. From a distance it looks like the only plant growing is grass, but closer examination reveals a culture unique to the prairie.

Our land. One part of the span of grass will yield rows of ripe golden grains. Another section will become our cluster of buildings. And a part will be left as native prairie to cut for winter forage. Even in its natural state it can provide food.

Samuel scrapes his boot heel into the moist earth to loosen the soil. Hunching down, he gathers a handful, squeezing it in his hand to feel the texture. The children move in close to see what will appear when he opens his hand. Tiny hands pull open Samuel's large fingers to see inside. He patiently explains that this very soil which we moved to America to find, will feed us and our livestock from now on. Josefina, whom I perch on my knee in front of Samuel, instinctively grabs at the soil to stuff it in her mouth. The children will be a part of this soil as much as we are.

We find the marker on the northwest corner and turn south. The range of buttes continue on the right side of us as far south as we can see. The two hills closest to us are about a mile away.

We walk south down a slight slope to find the next marker. Samuel hikes away from us, head fixed due south, counting his long strides. The land agent told him to look for the next marker at about a thousand steps from the first. The panoramic sky dwarfs the children and me as we meander down to meet him. Oscar and Emilia run, stop and inspect a buffalo skull, then dart to something else. I stroll down with Josefina on my hip, relaxed to see my family together on our land. Although it took a year longer than we planned, we are finally ready to plant our dreams in the soil of this prairie.

Samuel finds the two south points and we head back up the slope to the northeast corner. I pull a linen bag from our food basket. Our parents sent this sack with Mathilda, instructing us not to open it until the day we arrived on our new land. We do not know what the hard thing in the sack is, but it is so important that Mathilda carried it all the way from Sweden.

Inside, wrapped in paper, is a small packet of rye seed and a half-loaf of rock-hard bread. It puzzles us until I realize by its shape that it is the *såkaka,* the Christmas bread. Grain from the last sheaf of rye harvested from the field is ground into meal to bake this loaf. It has a place of honor on the Christmas table but is not eaten. It is wrapped and stored away until spring. When the earth warms up the soil for spring planting, the hard dry bread is pounded into bits. The crumbs are fed to the man and beast that are going to plant the new crop, and the rest is mixed with the seed that is being planted back into the earth. This magic food gives all involved the strength and vigor to start the new cycle of life.

This loaf was made from grain raised in Kulla on Samuel's ancestors' land. The grain was harvested by my *fader* and baked by my *moder*. They kept half the loaf to bless their spring crop and sent the other to us for good luck.

From one generation's homestead in Sweden, begins the next generation's farm in America.

I break off little pieces of bread for each of us to eat as symbols of the planter. We'll need strength and prayers to turn this prairie into a home.

At the northeast corner of our new land, the one closest to Sweden, Samuel pushes our new shovel into the ground and turns the first scoop of soil. Mixing some rubbed-off bread crumbs with the rye, I plant the seeds in the fresh-turned soil. Their Swedish roots will grow in American soil, just as our family plans to do.

When we come to this spot to check the rye's growth we can look toward the east to where we, and this blessing, came from— our parents and our native country of Sweden.

Glossary of Swedish Words

Amerikafeber: American fever

Arrendator: Tenant farmer

Brudkista: Bride's chest

Fader: Father

Farfar: Father's father, or fraternal grandfather

Farmor: Father's mother, or fraternal grandmother

Gök: Swedish cuckoo

Hemlängtan: Nostalgia, pining for home

Hemmansägare: Free farmer who owns his own farm

Julotta: Early-morning Christmas church service

Jultomte: Christmas elf that delivers presents

Kyrkonvården: Churchwarden

Lutfisk: Codfish usually served for Christmas Eve meal

Län: County

Moder: Mother

Morfar: Mother's father, or maternal grandfather

Mormor: Mother's mother, or maternal grandmother

Parastuga: Two-room house

Piga: Maidservant

Riksdaler: Swedish currency

Sill: Herring

Sillgata: Herring Street

Såkaka: Special Christmas bread made from the last grain harvested in the fall

Tomte: Mythical elf that protects Swedish homes

Undantag: To live as a former owner of a farm with certain rights to part of the yield of the farm

Vådträd: Ancestral tree on family farm

Family Charts

Samuel Amundsson Printz (1813-?)
Anna Lena Nilsdotter (1816-?)

Children and grandchildren known as of 1869:

1. Carolina Albertina Samuelsdotter (1842-1895?)
husband: Gustaf Otto Jonsson (1834-1864)
   1. Emelia Christina Gustafsdotter (1863-?)
husband: Johan Erik Jonsson (1843-?)
   2. Carolina Josefina Johandsdotter (1866-?)
   3. Julia Augusta Johansdotter (1869-?)

2. Christina Charlotta Samuelsdotter (1844-1919)
husband: Samuel Fredrik Johansson (1836-1919)
   1. Carl Johan Oscar Samuelson (1864-1935)
   2. Emilia Christina Samuelsdotter (1866-1943)
   3. Josefina Mathilda Johnson (1868-1869/70?)

3. Hedvig (Hedda) Samuelsdotter (1847-1916)

4. Mathilda Samuelsdotter (1850-1918)

5. Carl Johan Samuelsson (1853-1930)

6. Anna Sofia Samuelsdotter (1856-?)

7. Helen Maria Samuelsdotter (1862-1863)

Johannes Samuelsson (1788-1874)
Anna Greta Petersdotter (1798-1851)

Children and grandchildren known as of 1869:

1. Johan Petter Johansson (1817-1818)

2. Carl Johan Johansson (1819-?)

3. Carl Johan Johansson (1822-1822)

4. Carl Peter Johansson (1823-?)
wife: Stina Greta Andersdotter (1829-?)
    1. Emelia Christina Carlsdotter (1856-?)
    2. Carl Johan Oscar Carlsson (1859-?)
    3. Anna Carolina Carlsdotter (1861-?)

5. Anna Carolina Johansdotter (1826-1830)

6. Anders Johan Johansson (1830-?)

7. Bror August Theodor Johansson (1833-?)
wife: Christina Sofia Jonsdotter (1834-?)
    1. Augusta Christina Brorsdotter (1860-?)
    2. Johan August Wilhelm Brorsson (1862-?)
    3. Anna Carolina Brorsdotter (1864-?)

8. Ottilda Christina Charlotta Johansdotter (1835-1835)

9. Samuel Fredrik Johansson (1836-1919)
wife: Christina Charlotta Samuelsdotter (1844-1919)
    1. Carl Johan Oscar Samuelson (1864-1935)
    2. Emilia Christina Samuelsdotter (1866-1943)
    3. Josefina Mathilda Johnson (1868-1869/70?)

10. Mathilda Maria Christina Johansdotter (1840-?)

Johannes Samuelsson's second wife (sister of first wife)
Stina Cathrina Petersdotter (1807-1879)

Selected Bibliography

Andreas, A. T. *History of the State of Kansas.* Chicago, Ill.: A. T. Andreas, 1883.

Badger, David Alan, Crystle D. Clark, and Nancy A. Tellier. *Bishop Hill, Fifteen Years That Last Forever.* Havana, Ill.: Badger, 1996.

Barton, H. Arnold. *The Search for Ancestors: A Swedish-American Family Saga.* Carbondale: Southern Illinois University Press, 1979.

Barton, H. Arnold, ed. *Letters from the Promised Land: Swedes in America, 1840-1914.* Minneapolis: University of Minnesota Press, 1975.

Billdt, Ruth. *Pioneer Swedish-American Culture in Central Kansas.* Lindsborg, Kan.: Lindsborg News-Record, 1965.

Billdt, Ruth, and Elizabeth Jaderborg. *The Smoky Valley in the After Years.* Lindsborg, Kan.: Lindsborg News-Record, 1969.

Bojer, Johan. *The Emigrants.* Lincoln: University of Nebraska Press, 1978.

Deaths and Interments- Saline Co., Kansas 1859-1985. Compiled by the Smoky Valley Genealogical Society and Library Inc., 1985.

Dick, Everett. *The Sod-House Frontier 1854-1890.* Lincoln: University of Nebraska Press, 1989.

Dykstra, Robert R. *The Cattle Towns.* Lincoln: University of Nebraska Press, 1983.

Evitts, William J. *Early Immigration in the United States.* New York: Franklin Watts, 1989.

Fisher, Leonard Everett. *Tracks Across America*. New York: Holiday House, 1992.

Klein, Maury. *Union Pacific*. Garden City, New York: Doubleday & Co., Inc., 1987.

Holmquist, Thomas N. *Pioneer Cross*. Hillsboro, Kan.: Hearth Publishing, 1994.

Jacobs, William Jay. *Ellis Island: New Hope in a New Land*. New York: Charles Scribner's Sons, 1990.

Johansson, Carl-Erik. *Cradled in Sweden*. Logan, Utah: Everton Publishers, Inc., 1972.

Johnson, L. A. *The Augustana Synod: A Brief Review of its History*. Rock Island, Ill.: Augustana Book Concern, 1910.

Judson, Clara Ingram. *They Came from Sweden*. New York: Houghton Mifflin Company, 1942.

Lawlor, Veronia, ed. *I Was Dreaming to Come to America*. New York: Penguin, 1995.

Lindquist, Emory. *The Smoky Valley People: A History of Lindsborg, Kansas*. Rock Island, Ill.: Augustana Book Concern, 1953.

Lindsborg Efter Femtio År. Rock Island, Ill.: Augustana Book Concern, 1919.

Lindsborg pa Svensk-Amerikansk Kulturbild från Mellersta Kansas. Rock Island, Ill.: Augustana Book Concern, 1909.

Lorènzen, Lilly. *Of Swedish Ways*. Minneapolis: Dillon Press, Inc., 1964.

McGill, Allyson. *The Swedish Americans*. New York: Chelsea House Publishers, 1988.

Minnes Album—Svenska Lutherska Församlingen, Salemsborg, Kansas, 1869-1909. Rock Island, Ill.: Augustana Book Concern, 1909.

Moberg, Vilhelm. *The Emigrants*. New York: Simon and Schuster, 1951.

The Monitor Guide to Post Offices and Railroad Stations in the United States and Canada, 1876. New York: E. W. Bullinger, 1876.

Overton, Richard C. *Burlington Route.* New York: Alfred A. Knopf, 1965.

Pinzke, Nancy Lindberg. *Faces of Utopia.* Chicago, 1982.

Rockswold, E. Palmer. *Per, Immigrant and Pioneer.* Cambridge, Minn.: Adventure Publications, 1981.

Runblom, Harald, and Hans Norman, eds. *From Sweden to America: A History of the Migration.* Minneapolis: University of Minnesota Press, 1976.

Setterdahl, Lilly. *A Pioneer Lutheran Minister.* Andover, Ill.: The Jenny Lind Chapel Fund, 1986.

Swank, George. *Bishop Hill: Swedish-American Showcase.* Galva, Ill., 1965.

Vid Fyrtioårsfesten, Svenska Evangeliskt Lutherska Assaria Församlingen i Assaria, Kansas Den 6-8 Okt. 1916.

Wright, Robert L. *Swedish Emigrant Ballads.* Lincoln: University of Nebraska Press, 1965.

Books by Linda K. Hubalek

the *Butter in the Well* series

Butter in the Well

Read the endearing account of Kajsa Svensson Runeberg, an immigrant wife who recounts how she and
her family built up a farm on the unsettled prairie.

Quality soft book • $9.95 • ISBN 1-886652-00-7
6 x 9 • 144 pages
Abr. audio cassette • $9.95 • ISBN 1-886652-04-X
90 minutes

Prärieblomman

This tender, touching diary continues the saga of
Kajsa Runeberg's family through her daughter,
Alma, as she blossoms into a young woman.

Quality soft book • $9.95 • ISBN 1-886652-01-5
6 x 9 • 144 pages
Abr. audio cassette • $9.95 • ISBN 1-886652-05-8
90 minutes

Egg Gravy

Everyone who's ever treasured a family recipe or
marveled at the special touches Mother added to her
cooking will enjoy this collection of recipes and wis-
dom from the homestead family.

Quality soft book • $9.95 • ISBN 1-886652-02-3
6 x 9 • 136 pages

Looking Back

During her final week on the land she homesteaded,
Kajsa reminisces about the growth and changes she
experienced during her 51 years on the farm. Don't
miss this heart-touching finale!

Quality soft book • $9.95 • ISBN 1-886652-03-1
6 x 9 • 140 pages

(continued on next page)

***Butter in the Well* note cards**— Three full-color designs per package, featuring the family and farm.

***Homestead* note cards**—This full-color design shows the original homestead.

Either style of note card —$4.95/ set. Each set contains 6 cards and envelopes in a clear vinyl pouch. Each card: 5 1/2 x 4 1/4 inches.

Postcards— One full-color design of homestead. $3.95 for a packet of 12.

the *Trail of Thread series*

Trail of Thread

Taste the dust of the road and feel the wind in your face as you travel with a Kentucky family by wagon trail to the new territory of Kansas in 1854.

Quality soft book • $9.95 • ISBN 1-886652-06-6
6 x 9 • 124 pages

Thimble of Soil

Experience the terror of the fighting and the determination to endure as you stake a claim alongside the women caught in the bloody conflicts of Kansas in the 1850s.

Quality soft book • $9.95 • ISBN 1-886652-07-4
6 x 9 • 120 pages

Stitch of Courage

Face the uncertainty of the conflict and challenge the purpose of the fight with the women of Kansas during the Civil War.
Quality soft book • $9.95 • ISBN 1-886652-08-2
6 x 9 • 120 pages

Order Form

Book Kansas!/Butterfield Books
P.O. Box 407
Lindsborg, KS 67456
1-800-790-2665

SEND TO:

Name _____

Address _____

City _____

State _____ Zip _____

Phone # _____

☐ Check enclosed for entire amount payable to
Butterfield Books

☐ Visa   ☐ MasterCard

Card # [ ][ ][ ][ ] [ ][ ][ ][ ] [ ][ ][ ][ ] [ ][ ][ ][ ]

Exp Date [ ][ ]

Signature (or call to place your order) _____ Date _____

ISBN #	TITLE	QTY	UNIT PRICE	TOTAL
1-886652-00-7	Butter in the Well		9.95	
1-886652-01-5	Prärieblomman		9.95	
1-886652-02-3	Egg Gravy		9.95	
1-886652-03-1	Looking Back		9.95	
1-886652-04-X	**Cassette:** Butter in the Well		9.95	
1-886652-05-8	**Cassette:** Prärieblomman		9.95	
	Note cards: Butter in the Well		4.95	
	Note cards: Homestead		4.95	
	Postcards: Homestead		3.95	
1-886652-06-6	Trail of Thread		9.95	
1-886652-07-4	Thimble of Soil		9.95	
1-886652-08-2	Stitch of Courage		9.95	
1-886652-11-2	Planting Dreams		9.95	
1-886652-12-0	Cultivating Hope (Fall 1998)		9.95	
1-886652-13-9	Harvesting Faith (Fall 1999)		9.95	
			Subtotal	
			KS add 6.4% tax	
Shipping & Handling: per address ($3.00 for first item. Each additional item .50)				
			Total	

Retailers and Libraries: Books are available through Butterfield Books, B & T, Booksource and Ingram.
RIF Programs and Schools: Contact Butterfield Books for discount, ordering and author appearances.

Order Form

Book Kansas!/Butterfield Books
P.O. Box 407
Lindsborg, KS 67456
1-800-790-2665

SEND TO:

Name _____

Address _____

City _____

State _____ Zip _____

Phone # _____

☐ Check enclosed for entire amount payable to
   Butterfield Books

☐ Visa ☐ MasterCard

Card # ☐☐☐☐ ☐☐☐☐ ☐☐☐☐ ☐☐☐☐

Exp Date ☐☐☐

Signature (or call to place your order) _____ Date _____

ISBN #	TITLE	QTY	UNIT PRICE	TOTAL
1-886652-00-7	Butter in the Well		9.95	
1-886652-01-5	Prärieblomman		9.95	
1-886652-02-3	Egg Gravy		9.95	
1-886652-03-1	Looking Back		9.95	
1-886652-04-X	**Cassette:** Butter in the Well		9.95	
1-886652-05-8	**Cassette:** Prärieblomman		9.95	
	Note cards: Butter in the Well		4.95	
	Note cards: Homestead		4.95	
	Postcards: Homestead		3.95	
1-886652-06-6	Trail of Thread		9.95	
1-886652-07-4	Thimble of Soil		9.95	
1-886652-08-2	Stitch of Courage		9.95	
1-886652-11-2	Planting Dreams		9.95	
1-886652-12-0	Cultivating Hope (Fall 1998)		9.95	
1-886652-13-9	Harvesting Faith (Fall 1999)		9.95	
			Subtotal	
			KS add 6.4% tax	
Shipping & Handling: per address ($3.00 for first item. Each additional item .50)				
			Total	

Retailers and Libraries: Books are available through Butterfield Books, B & T, Booksource and Ingram.
RIF Programs and Schools: Contact Butterfield Books for discount, ordering and author appearances.

About the Author

A door may close in your life but a window will open instead.

Linda Hubalek knew years ago she wanted to write a book someday about her great-grandmother, Kizzie Pieratt, but it took a major move in her life to point her toward her new career in writing.

Hubalek's chance came unexpectedly when her husband was transferred from his job in the Midwest to the West Coast. She had to sell her wholesale floral business and find a new career.

Homesick for her family and the farmland of the Midwest, she turned to writing about what she missed, and the inspiration was kindled to write about her ancestors and the land they homesteaded.

What resulted was the *Butter in the Well* series, four books based on the Swedish immigrant woman who homesteaded the family farm in Kansas where Hubalek grew up.

In her second series, *Trail of Thread*, Hubalek follows her maternal ancestors, who traveled to Kansas in the 1850s. These three books relive the turbulent times the pioneer women faced before and during the Civil War.

Planting Dreams, her third series, portrays Hubalek's great-great-grandmother, who left Sweden in 1868 to find land in America. These three books trace her family's journey to Kansas and the homesteading of their farm.

Linda Hubalek lives in the Midwest again, close to the roots of her writing career.

The author loves to hear from her readers. You may write to her in care of Butterfield Books, Inc., PO Box 407, Lindsborg, KS 67456-0407.